SPECIAL MESSAGE TO READERS

This book is published by

THE ULVERSCROFT FOUNDATION

a registered charity in the U.K., No. 264873

The Foundation was established in 1974 to provide funds to help towards research, diagnosis and treatment of eye diseases. Below are a few examples of contributions made by THE ULVERSCROFT FOUNDATION:

A new Children's Assessment Unit
at Moorfield's Hospital, London.

•

Twin operating theatres at the
Western Ophthalmic Hospital, London.

•

The Frederick Thorpe Ulverscroft Chair of
Ophthalmology at the University of Leicester.

•

Eye Laser equipment to various eye hospitals.

If you would like to help further the work of the Foundation by making a donation or leaving a legacy, every contribution, no matter how small, is received with gratitude. Please write for details to:

THE ULVERSCROFT FOUNDATION,
**The Green, Bradgate Road, Anstey,
Leicester LE7 7FU. England
Telephone: (0533) 364325**

Love is
a time of enchantment:
in it all days are fair and all fields
green. Youth is blest by it,
old age made benign: the eyes of love see
roses blooming in December,
and sunshine through rain. Verily
is the time of true-love
a time of enchantment — and
Oh! how eager is woman
to be bewitched!

A DISTANT HOPE

To Andria Vincent, a rising young actress, the future looks rosy. She is beautiful, talented and in love. But one dreadful morning an unexpected discovery shatters her world. Then Ellard Ashton offers her a part in a play he is promoting. Listlessly she accepts. Meanwhile, Ellard is becoming more than a friend, but just how far can she trust him and her own uncertain heart?

SYLVIA E. KIRK

◆

A
DISTANT HOPE

Complete and Unabridged

ULVERSCROFT
Leicester

First published in Great Britain in 1988 by
Robert Hale Limited
London

First Large Print Edition
published February 1991
by arrangement with
Robert Hale Limited
London

British Library CIP Data

Kirk, Sylvia E.
 A distant hope. — Large print ed. —
Ulverscroft large print series: romance
I. Title
823'.914   [F]

ISBN 0–7089–2369–0

Published by
F. A. Thorpe (Publishing) Ltd.
Anstey, Leicestershire
Set by Words & Graphics Ltd.
Anstey, Leicestershire
Printed and bound in Great Britain by
T. J. Press (Padstow) Ltd., Padstow, Cornwall

1

OUTSIDE a car horn sounded impatiently, and Andria picked up her suitcase and went quickly down the narrow stairs, calling goodbye to her flatmate as she went. Suky came out on the landing and waved her goodbye. Andria closed the door behind her, then gasped with surprise. Instead of the broken-down old car she had expected, Oliver was sitting behind the wheel of a new looking Fiat, smirking complacently.

"Hop in, darling," he said, pushing the door open for her. "You look scrumptious."

"Thanks, but where did you get this?" she asked, as he heaved her suitcase into the back seat. "Did you hire it?"

"Borrowed it from a friend," Oliver grinned. "I told him I was desperate to impress my girl's mother, and he took pity and lent it to me. You must admit it's an improvement on Emily."

"Anything's an improvement on Emily!" Andria said feelingly. "Oliver, Constance

1

won't mind what you're driving, she never takes any notice of things like that. She'll be far more interested in your acting ability, believe me."

"Let's hope that producer friend of hers is, too," Oliver said, as they moved slowly out of the mews. "I'm sick of being an out-of-work actor."

He smiled as he spoke, but Andria knew that he was desperately serious — apart from some modelling and advertising work which he had only accepted to pay his bills, Oliver hadn't worked for nearly a year. As he had said himself, it was high time his career took off.

She put her hand over his for a moment, and he turned his over and squeezed hers, then swore under his breath as a taxi brushed past them with inches to spare.

"Sorry, Andy, I must concentrate," he said. "I promised Charlie I'd return his car unblemished, so I've got to be careful. Besides, it wouldn't look so good if I turned up at your mother's with a dirty great rip in it, would it?"

"No," Andria admitted, and straightened in her seat, her mind travelling to her mother . . . would Constance be able to

2

help? *Would* she help? Usually she was kind in a casual sort of way, but just occasionally she could take a dislike to a person, and then they might as well take themselves out of her sight and never come back, because nothing would change her opinion.

"I hope she likes Oliver," Andria thought. "She *must* like him, she must . . . "

"Do you know this producer guy?" Oliver asked, and Andria shook her head.

"No, not personally, but I've heard of him," she said. "He's been in the States for a long time, then he came back and Constance told me he's got three theatres on the go, two in London and one in Manchester. I think he was quite successful in America."

"Well, let's hope he's successful here too," Oliver said. "I must say I haven't heard too much about him — what was his name again? Ellard Ashton?"

"That's right. According to Constance he isn't very old, in his early thirties."

"I'll be thirty in two years time," Oliver said in a hollow voice. "Andy, I've got to make a go of something, I've *got* to."

"You will." She squeezed his elbow,

almost feeling his tension, but she said nothing, knowing that when he was like this he couldn't even take sympathy . . .

"Tell me who else will be there," Oliver said, and Andria frowned, trying to remember.

"Well, Constance of course, and Ellard Ashton, and I think the man who wrote one of the plays he's putting on — Michael Lester, and one or two others, I'm not quite sure who. But it will be all right, I know it will — you're a great actor."

"Let's hope they all think so," Oliver said, and managed a tight little smile. "Tell me about the house."

She had already described it to him, but she told him again, patiently, how Constance had seen three tumbledown cottages and had engaged an architect friend to convert them into one extremely attractive house, with large beautiful gardens. Whether Constance would still be living there in a few years time was debatable, she had owned four different houses to Andria's knowledge, but at the moment she seemed quite happy with what she'd got . . .

"How old is your mother?" Oliver asked

4

suddenly, and Andria blinked.

"Well, I suppose she must be — she must be about thirty-seven, I suppose, but she doesn't look it."

"Judging from her photographs, no she doesn't," Oliver agreed. "She must have been very young when you were born."

"She was eighteen and on tour," Andria smiled. "So I really was born near the smell of grease paint."

"You're a pretty good actress yourself," Oliver said abruptly, and Andria's teeth caught in her bottom lip, because she had been lucky recently in her career, far luckier than Oliver . . .

"Thank you, sir," she said lightly. "I aim to please."

"Yes, you do, don't you?" Oliver shot her a faintly brooding glance from under his dark straight brows. "I bet your mother isn't so complaisant."

"Constance is a truly great actress," Andria said quietly. "If I get to be half as good as she is I'll be satisfied."

"Well, you've got a long way to go yet," Oliver smiled suddenly, as if his despondent mood had suddenly lifted. "But I think you'll get there."

"We'll get there together," Andria said, and he laughed and pressed her hand again.

The sprawl of London fell away, and the sun came out from behind the clouds and shone palely on the fields and woods on either side of the road. It was too early in the year for it to have any strength, but it was cheering and Andria felt her spirits lift. Of course it would be all right, Constance would help Oliver as soon as she recognised his talent — she had helped other people, and when she realised how much it meant to both of them she would be eager to do what she could. And Constance could do a great deal, far more than Andria herself, however much she loved Oliver.

"Which turning?" Oliver asked suddenly, and Andria jerked herself away from her thoughts.

"The next one, to the left," she said, and Oliver moved smoothly into the left-hand traffic lane.

"You drive very well, darling," Andria said, and Oliver gave a self-satisfied little smirk.

"Cars and women, you have to know how to handle them," he said outrageously, and

6

Andria thumped him, laughing.

But as they drew nearer their destination, her heart began to beat a little faster. Everything depended on first impressions — Constance disliked very handsome men, she thought they were conceited, she didn't mind casual clothes but she hated sloppy or grubby ones, she didn't mind confident people but she detested cocksure ones . . .

Andria looked sideways at Oliver, noting his dark curling hair, just the right length, his long eyelashes, his firm chin and rather prominent nose . . . nice-looking but not *too* handsome — just right, in fact . . .

"Now down this lane to the right," she said aloud, and Oliver turned obediently, his hands firm and competent on the wheel.

The white painted house with the long thatched roof came in sight, and Andria drew a ragged breath. The next few minutes could be crucial . . .

The big farm gates were open, and Oliver went slowly up the drive-in, past the shrubs which were already in bud, and after a few moments the house came in view. Oliver stopped the car and surveyed it for a moment.

"It's just like an overgrown country cottage," he commented.

"Well, that's what it is, really," Andria smiled to conceal her nervousness. "Come on, darling, let's get out."

She fumbled in her handbag for the key, but just as they reached the front door it opened and Constance stood there, framed in the opening, tall and graceful, smiling a welcome.

"Andy, darling!" she cried, holding out her arms, and Andy went into her scented embrace with an inward sigh of relief. Her mother was in a good mood. . . .

"Constance, this is Oliver," Andria said as soon as she was released. "Darling, this is my mother."

There was a long pause, while Constance looked him over, her amber eyes slightly narrowed. Then she smiled and held out her hand.

"So you're the famous Oliver," she said. "I've heard a great deal about you from Andy."

"More than enough, Miss Vincent," Oliver said, smiling in his turn. "It's very good of you to invite me for the weekend."

8

"Call me Constance, everybody does, and do come in and put those suitcases down . . . Did you have a good journey?"

"Very good," Andria replied. "Who's here?"

"Not many people, darling," Constance led the way upstairs, talking over her shoulder. "Ellard Ashton, of course, and Michael Lester and his wife — she's a delightful girl, very interested in gardening, and yourselves, and that's it . . . This is your room, Oliver, and you've got your usual one, Andy. Hurry up and come down, we were just going to have coffee."

She turned and left them, and Oliver looked after her and gave a long soundless whistle.

"Well, she — she's really something, isn't she?" he said quietly. "Now I know where you got your looks from."

"Flatterer." Andria reached up and kissed him quickly. "Don't be long, will you? Constance hates to be kept waiting."

"Oh, right."

Oliver disappeared with his suitcase, and Andria went into the familiar bedroom, closing the door behind her.

It was just the same — the white

9

wardrobes, the thick carpet, the dolls she had never really wanted sitting on the window sill, dolls from every country Constance had visited, brought home for the little girl who would rather have had her mother permanently with her . . .

Andria dumped her things on the bed, combed her hair hastily, washed her hands and went out, just in time to meet Oliver emerging from his room, looking a trifle apprehensive.

"They're all down there, then," he said under his breath. "The producer and the writer both — this could be *it*, Andy."

"Yes, it could." She smiled encouragingly at him. "Come on, I'm sure it's going to be all right."

They went downstairs together, Andria slightly in the lead, and pushed open the lounge door.

Constance was leaning against the piano, a cup in her hand, talking animatedly to the three other people in the room, a tall thin man with fair hair and a thin, intelligent face, a pretty young woman with curly dark hair, and a broad-shouldered man who was seated at the piano as if about to play it.

"Come in, darlings," Constance smiled

widely. "People, this is my daughter, Andy, and this is Oliver, her — her friend. Andy, this is Michael, who's written this terribly clever play we're all so interested in, this is Polly who knows all about plants and is teaching me, and this is Ellard, who's having the good sense to put the play on."

"It's nonsense to say I know all about plants," Polly rose, offering her hand and laughing. "Your mother knows far more than I do."

"It's Constance's hobby," Andria said. "You're obviously a fellow enthusiast."

"I think she's made a wonderful job of the garden," Polly said. "Don't you, Ellard?"

Andria turned to shake hands with him, and was conscious of searching dark eyes travelling deliberately all over her, while a hard hand held hers in a close grip.

"You're very like your mother, aren't you?" Ellard Ashton said. "You must be proud of her, Con."

"Oh, I am," Constance smiled. "Now who takes white coffee and who takes black?"

"Black, please." Oliver seated himself

beside Polly, who moved along the settee to make room for him. "This is a nice room, Constance."

"I like it," Constance smiled. "What do you think of the big windows? Somebody said they were out of keeping with the rest of the house, but I wanted a good view of the garden. A biscuit, Michael?"

"Please." He took one with a grin, shy and rather endearing. "Polly thinks I ought to be fatter."

"He eats like a horse and just look at him!" Polly said sadly.

"Artists should be skinny," Constance declared. "Whoever heard of a fat genius?"

"What's your play about?" Andria asked Michael, but before he could reply Constance interrupted.

"Not now, darling, we're relaxing today. I'll give you both a copy of the script tonight so you can read it in bed."

"Well, that's a step forward," Andria thought, and shot Oliver an encouraging glance. He smiled briefly, sipping his coffee, and Ellard started to describe an incident which had happened to him on his way down from the north. Andria only half listened, her thoughts were with

Oliver — would there be a part in the play for him or had Ellard cast it already? Constance hadn't said so but it was possible, and if so then Oliver was going to be sickeningly disappointed . . . unless, of course, there was another production in the pipeline, which there might be.

A few minutes later Constance shepherded them all outside, and they wandered about, inspecting her garden. Oliver said all the right things, falling in step with his hostess, while Andria found herself walking next to Ellard Ashton.

"So your young friend wants a part in my play," he said abruptly, and Andria's stomach contracted.

"Yes," she said, breathlessly. "Yes, he — he does, Ellard, if — if it's possible."

"We'll see," Ellard said, still abruptly. "You can do a scene for me together tomorrow after you've had a chance to study the script, and if he's any good I'll think about it."

"Thank you," Andria said sincerely. "Thank you very much."

He looked at her, a light frown between his brows, then nodded and changing the subject completely, asked if she knew the

13

name of the shrub he was standing next to.

"I think it's a weigela," Andria said. "It has red or pink flowers later on, rather nice."

"M'm." They strolled on, and Ellard asked where she lived.

"I share a flat with my friend Suky," Andria told him. "She's a nurse at a big hospital, but I think she'll be moving soon. She's getting married later on this year, to an airline pilot."

"I see," Ellard nodded. "I suppose the rent is pretty steep?"

"It's horrendous," Andria said. "But I've been quite lucky lately, and then Constance insists on giving me an allowance, which I don't really need, so we manage very well."

"Generous Constance," Ellard said, smiling.

The smile lit up his rather stern face, and she found herself suddenly wondering how old he was and what he was really like as a person. Obviously he must have a great deal of drive and initiative, or he would not be in the position he was, and he must have intuition as well . . .

"You're very fond of him, aren't you?" Ellard asked suddenly, and Andria nodded.

"M'm," Ellard nodded. "Well, we'll see . . .

She had to be content with that, realising that it would do no good to press the point, and they strolled on, until Constance declared that she was starving and they would go inside for lunch.

It was typical of Constance that she had found someone locally who was an excellent cook, Andria thought as she munched her way appreciatively through a first-class meal. But then Constance always paid for what she wanted so why not?

In the afternoon they all went riding, mounted on horses from a local stables, and Andria was surprised to discover that Oliver was nervous of horses, though he concealed it very well. Ellard on the other hand looked perfectly at home in the saddle, and as they trotted side by side along a country lane she asked where he had learned.

"In the States," he said curtly, and changed the subject.

The ride over, to Oliver's relief,

Constance decided that they would go home and have toasted crumpets for tea.

"Oh, Constance, they're fattening!" Andria moaned.

"Nonsense, that's all in the mind," Constance said briskly. "And anyway, I'm starving after all that exercise — you didn't do too badly for a beginner, Oliver."

"Thanks," Oliver smiled. "To be truthful, I was thrown from a horse once and broke my wrist — I've been a bit wary of them ever since."

"You poor pet, you should have said!" Constance exclaimed. "Andy, dear, why didn't you tell me Oliver didn't like horses?"

"I didn't know," Andria said truthfully.

It was a silly little incident, but for some reason it upset her, because somehow it seemed to emphasise Oliver's occasional lack of openness, in contrast to her own outgoing personality. He gave her an apologetic little smile, as if he read her thoughts.

"Well, never mind, you got on a horse again, so you're halfway to being cured," Polly said. "Brr, it's getting cold, can we hurry?"

16

"Let's run," Constance said, catching Oliver's hand, and they scampered away, leaving the rest of the party to follow at a more sober pace.

"I think your mother's taken to your boy-friend," Michael said, with his half shy engaging smile. "That's good, it does make things more pleasant, doesn't it?"

It did, and Andria's spirits rose again. She could hear Constance and Oliver laughing as they ran, and Polly fell into step with her, looking as if she wanted to say something. Ellard moved to walk beside Michael, and Polly said quietly:

"You were nervous, weren't you? It's awful bringing a guy home for the first time — I remember how scared I was that my parents wouldn't like Michael, but fortunately they did. Is he the first?"

"The first important one," Andria said, and Polly looked thoughtful.

"He's attractive, isn't he? Is he a good actor? Really good, I mean, because Michael's play — well, it does call for good performances, it won't be exactly easy to interpret, at least I don't think it will."

"He's a *very* good actor," Andria said

staunchly, stifling a little squirm of doubt. "He is, Polly."

"That's good," Polly nodded. "I'll be glad to get out of these breeches, I know I'm too fat for them!"

"No you're not," Andria felt a surge of affection for her. "You're just right . . . and it is getting cold, perhaps we should run too."

They found Constance and Oliver panting in the front porch, still laughing, and Andy said:

"Come on, Constance, we're freezing — can't you find your key?"

"I hate the way everyone assumes I'm completely *scatty,*" Constance said, holding it up between her finger and thumb and waving it under her daughter's nose. "Here it is, you disrespectful brat . . . ooh, that's better . . . "

They trooped into the house, and Andria heaved a sigh of relief. The wind had changed while they were out, and as she went upstairs to change she wondered if they were going to have some snow. She asked Oliver what he thought, but he shook his head.

"The sky hasn't got quite the right

18

leaden quality," he said as he went into his room to change. "Rain, perhaps."

Andria took off her riding things, tidied herself quickly and went downstairs, and discovered her mother kneeling in front of the log fire, toasting crumpets with a long-handled toasting fork. She looked up with a quick smile.

"You look nice, darling," she said. "That blue thing suits you, it matches your eyes . . . Is Oliver coming? I thought we'd have tea in here, it's much more comfortable. You know, I do think coal is better for toasting things over, don't you? Oh, here's Polly and Michael . . . "

It was a satisfying sort of day, Andria thought as she got ready for bed. True to her word, Constance had given her a copy of Michael's script to read, and she plumped up her pillows, wondering if Oliver was doing the same, and started to read.

It was a clever play, a mystery of sorts but with all kinds of nuances, and she saw at once what Polly meant — it would take skilled actors to make anything of it. She read it until her eyelids dropped and she yawned uncontrollably, then switched off her bedside lamp and went to sleep almost at once.

The next morning it was obvious that Constance's mood had changed. She was the actress now, not the attentive hostess, and after breakfast she ordered everyone into the lounge, where they discovered that she had moved all the furniture out of the way so that Oliver could play a scene from the play for them.

"We'll give him a real test, shall we, Ellard?" Constance said with a smile. "How about the scene where Paul realises his stepdaughter may have seen him kill his aunt?"

"Why not?" Oliver said, and there was a faint sparkle in his eye as if he meant to rise to the challenge. "Andria, will you be my stepdaughter? You're the youngest person here."

"All right," she agreed, and taking a deep breath, walked over to the fireplace and stood staring down at the flames, mentally switching herself into the part — a sulky, frightened adolescent, not quite sure of what she has seen or how to use the information to her own ends . . .

"Oh, here you are, Megan," Oliver said, and she turned slowly and gave him a hostile, brooding glance . . .

He did it very well, Andria thought, and she sensed that their audience was listening intently, until Polly, who had been roped in to play the housekeeper, interrupted them in time to stop Megan accusing him or Paul denying complicity . . .

There were a few minutes silence, then Ellard said quietly:

"Yes, I think so, don't you, Constance? Be at rehearsals next week." His gaze went to Andria, and she saw that he was frowning thoughtfully. "You had a very good supporting actress, didn't you? Well done, Andria."

She felt herself flush, then glanced at Oliver, whose face was breaking into a delighted smile.

"Thanks," he said. "Thanks, Ellard — and thank *you*, Constance."

"My dear, it was a pleasure," Constance beamed at everyone. Well, now that's over, we can all relax — how about a walk? It's a *glorious* morning."

Andria ran upstairs on winged feet, Oliver pounding up behind her, and on the landing he caught her round the waist and hugged her to him. They kissed, rubbing noses idiotically, until Andria broke away, pounding him with excitement.

"I told you, I *told* you!" she exclaimed. "Didn't I?"

"Yes, you did, you little wonder," Oliver laughed breathlessly and pulled her into his arms again. "You did it!"

"No, I didn't," Andria laughed back. "It was you — you're a good actor, Oliver, I always *knew* you were! I wonder what part they'll give you?"

"I don't much mind, to be honest," Oliver said frankly. "They're all pretty good and I can hardly expect the lead, can I? Rehearsals next week — Andy, I can't wait!"

"You haven't got long," she pointed out. "Con said it would be Wednesday."

"Come on, you two," Constance was calling from the hall. "We'll lose the sunshine!"

"Coming," Andria called back, and she and Oliver broke apart reluctantly.

They tramped through a nearby beech wood, Constance and Oliver leading the way, and as she watched them deep in animated conversation Andria thought how stupid she had been to worry that her mother might take a dislike to Oliver — obviously the reverse had happened, and she smiled to herself.

"Penny for them," Ellard said from her side, and she looked up at him with another quick smile.

"It's just that things seem to be working out so well," she said. "I was very apprehensive and I needn't have been, need I?"

There was a pause before he replied, then he said:

"Evidently not," in a curiously expressionless tone.

"Have you — have you decided what part you might give Oliver?" she asked, and Ellard shook his head.

"Not yet," he said. "There are two I'm considering, but we'll see . . . What are you doing at the moment, Andria?"

"Nothing, but I've been offered something in a fortnight's time, a small part in a TV play," she told him. "I think I'll take it."

He nodded, and she shot him a curious glance. He was frowning a little, as if something was puzzling him, then his brow cleared and he pointed something out to her — a small plant just breaking into flower. She bent over it obediently, and Polly and Michael joined them, looking too.

"It's wood sorrel," Polly said, after a moment. "Oh, look, we're getting left behind — come on, I wouldn't like to be lost in these woods."

She and Michael hurried after Constance and Oliver, and as he straightened up Ellard said abruptly:

"When are you going back to London, Andria?"

"I don't know exactly," Andria felt surprised. "Tonight or tomorrow, I suppose."

"Take my advice and make it tonight," Ellard said, and walked on.

Andria fell into step with him, feeling distinctly puzzled. What difference could it possibly make when they went back, provided Oliver turned up for rehearsals on Wednesday? Her lips parted to ask him, but there was something forbidding about the profile turned to her, and the words died unspoken.

2

POLLY and Michael left late that afternoon, driving away with Constance waving an almost tragic farewell.

"They're darlings, those two," she exclaimed as they disappeared from sight. "Ellard, we *must* have a success with Michael's play, we *must* . . . "

He gave her an amused little glance, his lips twitching.

"We will," he promised, and then he glanced at his watch, his eyebrows lifting a little.

"Con, I'll have to go myself soon," he said. "Well, all right, some tea then . . . "

"I can't see why you have to go to Manchester at all," Constance said, as she went into the kitchen. "Such a *dreary* place!"

"I do have a theatre there," he reminded her drily, and she pulled a face and disappeared.

Andria followed her, and found her mother not filling a kettle, but sitting on the edge of the table, a brooding expression on her lovely face.

"Is something the matter, Constance?" Andria asked, and her mother stared blankly at her for a moment, then smiled.

"No, I just hate goodbyes, that's all," she said. "Stupid of me . . . darling, see if there are any biscuits left, will you? Ellard has a frightfully long drive, he'll be starving by the time he gets there.

She slid off the table and picked up the kettle, and as she stood with her back to Andria she asked abruptly:

"Darling, you don't mind me asking, but are you and Oliver — are you actually lovers or just extremely good friends?"

"Extremely good friends, but I do love him," Andria replied.

Constance nodded slowly, gave a little sigh, and took the biscuit barrel from Andria.

"Why — why did you ask?" Andria said, a little puzzled. Constance was extremely casual about her daughter's love life, and apart from making sure that she knew enough to prevent unwanted pregnancies or any other social disaster, left her to live her own life.

"Oh, I just wondered," Constance smiled suddenly. "No real reason, darling . . . Do you want tea too?

"Yes, please.!"

Still puzzled, she picked up the tea tray and followed Constance into the lounge.

Oliver and Ellard were both there, Ellard standing with one elbow on the mantelpiece, Oliver sitting on the settee with his arms round his knees, a favourite position of his.

"I must say I do like staying here," Oliver observed with a cheeky grin. "The service is so good!"

"Any more sauce like that and you do the washing up," Constance said, smiling. "Do sit down, Ellard, you're wearing a hole in the woodwork with your elbow!"

He complied, flashing her a smile which transformed his rather grim face, and it was then that Andria noticed a small white scar on his upper lip, and wondered how he had got it.

He drank his tea quickly, refused biscuits and got up.

"I must go, Con," he said regretfully. "It's been a most enjoyable weekend. Andria, I'm glad to have met you. Oliver, don't be late on Wednesday, will you? I'll just go up and collect my case."

"I'll give you a hand," Oliver said, and followed him out of the room.

"I suppose we must see him off, too," Constance said, and got up in her turn.

It was cold on the doorstep, and Andria was glad when Ellard's car disappeared and they could return to the warmth of the house. Constance hugged her shapely arms, shivering.

"Well, that's that," she said. "Now we can close the door and be just ourselves ... Andy, darling, I've been thinking — you and Oliver don't have to go back tonight, do you? Why not stay for another day or two? I'm not doing anything in particular and the fresh air will do you good."

"There's certainly plenty of that," Oliver commented, as he closed the door behind them. "Andy, we could stay, couldn't we?"

"Yes, of course, if that's all right with you, Constance," Andria agreed, and her mother gave her a little sideways smile.

"I wouldn't have suggested it if it wasn't," she said gently, and Andria grinned, remembering the times she had been shooed out of the house because

Constance was working on some part and needed her privacy . . .

"That's settled, then," Constance said briskly, and led the way back to the lounge.

The next day Andria was despatched to do the shopping, while Oliver found himself in the garden, being taught how to prune roses by Constance, whose role seemed to have changed again to that of a country housewife, intent on keeping her garden nicely.

The village was some way away, but Andria had no difficulty in parking Constance's small car, and she had been furnished with a shopping list. She enjoyed herself wandering along the main street, in and out of small old-fashioned shops and newer, larger modern ones, and it was some time before she finished her purchases and went back to the car. As she started the engine, she thought suddenly of Oliver, and grinned. Poor Oliver, who hardly knew the top of a plant from the roots! How meekly he had agreed to help . . . But then, people did do what Constance asked — there was something about her forceful personality which ensured that . . .

She parked the car outside the front door, gathered up her bags and rang the bell. Constance came to the door, her hair ruffled, a pair of secateurs clutched in her hand.

"Goodness, darling, you are loaded!" she exclaimed. "Here, let me help you . . . bring it into the kitchen, we were going to have coffee in there, you're just in time."

Oliver was inside, perched on a kitchen stool, watching the coffee bubbling gently, while a delicious smell scented the air. He greeted Andria with a grin.

"I can prune three different kinds of roses now," he said smugly. "Aren't I clever?"

"Brilliant, darling," Andria laughed, kissing him. "Doesn't that smell *wonderful?* I'm really *ready* for that. That beastly wind is getting up again."

"I know," Constance smoothed her Titian mane. "That's why we came in . . . Don't say you forgot the apples . . . no, you didn't, here they are . . . and the peppers, good."

"Con's going to cook us something

strange and exotic for dinner tonight," Oliver said, as Constance poured their coffee. "If you'd forgotten the peppers it would have been a domestic disaster."

"I am not," Andria said with mock dignity, "in the habit of forgetting . . . ooh, thanks, Con."

"I've been thinking," Constance said abruptly. "Why don't we go into Brighton this afternoon? It's quite a nice place if you ignore that dreadful Pavilion."

"Won't it be cold?" Andria asked. "I mean, I'd quite like to, but won't it?"

"We can wrap up," Constance said, and that appeared to be that . . .

It may have been the sea air, but that evening Andria could hardly keep her eyes open, and when Oliver hid his third yawn behind his hand she stood up regretfully.

"I'm sorry, Constance, but I'm too tired to be interesting to anyone anymore," she said apologetically. "Would you mind if I went to bed now? I should pack up tonight if we're going to make an early start in the morning."

"So should I." Oliver yawned again, openly this time.

"I suppose it is getting late," Constance stretched like a lovely, lazy cat. "All right, then, see you both in the morning."

Andria kissed her mother's silky cheek and went upstairs, followed by Oliver. Outside her door they kissed, a little sleepily, and Andria whispered:

"It's been a success, hasn't it? Are you glad you came?"

"You bet your sweet life I am." He hugged her hard, his lips on her hair. "Night, Andy, I'm out on my feet . . . "

He smiled blearily at her and went into his room, closing the door behind him, and she wondered suddenly if now he would consider putting their friendship on a different sort of footing . . . he might now that he was happier about his career, and as she packed her suitcase, forcing herself to concentrate on the task, she began to wonder if when Suky got married and left the flat, Oliver could be persuaded to move in . . . or perhaps another flat, a bigger one . . .

She got into bed, smiling happily to herself, wondering if Oliver would want them to get married. So far he had shown himself surprisingly conventional for an actor, so perhaps he would prefer that to their simply living together . . .

She closed her eyes, wriggled into a comfortable position, and let herself drift into sleep . . .

Somewhere through her dreams she heard a door open and close, and guessed that Constance had come to bed. Dear Constance, how kind and helpful she had been . . .

Andria woke early the next morning, and for a moment did not realise where she was. The sun was streaming through the window, and when she reached for the bedside clock she saw that it was nearly seven. Would Constance like an early morning cup of tea, Andria wondered? When she was a little girl she had done this for her mother, creeping upstairs with a tray, not quite sure of her reception. A careful placing of the tray, a timid tap on the door, and Constance's sleepy voice calling:

"Come in, whoever it is . . . oh, darling, you shouldn't have . . . how nice . . . biscuits, too!"

Smiling at the memory Andria padded

33

quietly into the bathroom, showered quickly and dressed, then went downstairs to the kitchen. This might be an opportunity to tell her mother just how grateful she was to her for helping Oliver.

She made the tea, arranged cups and saucers on it, found the biscuit tin, put fresh milk in the jug and started upstairs, moving quietly to avoid spilling anything. She smiled again, remembering herself as a child, tongue slightly protruding in an effort at concentration, stepping laboriously from stair to stair, pausing to take a firmer grip on the laden tray.

She put it down on the carpet outside Constance's door, tapped once, opened the door and went inside, pushing it to with her elbow. There was space for the tray on the bedside table, and she walked over to the bed. As she did so the long shape which was her mother moved suddenly under the bedclothes and sat up in one rapid movement, eyes wide in the dim light of the bedroom.

"Andria!" she gasped, and there was an equally sudden movement beside her.

A hand appeared, then a tousled dark head, and there was Oliver, blinking with disturbed sleep, staring as he realised that Andria was there, staring back at him in horrified disbelief. For a moment they stayed frozen, then Andria gave a choked cry, the tray slipped to the floor with a muted crash, tea and milk spilling over the thick carpet, and she was running from the room as if devil pursued, running into her own bedroom, seizing her suitcase, throwing handfuls of her belongings into it, wrenching it closed, tearing down the stairs and out of the house.

As she pounded down the drive-in she thought she heard her mother calling out to her, but she sped on, the suitcase hampering her movements, tears streaking down her face. "The station," she thought. "Get away from here — get away . . . "

Her arms were aching and her legs felt like lead when she finally arrived at the little country railway station, and as she grovelled in her purse for the fare back to London her fingers shook with cold. She felt icy all over, cold and sick, and as she hurried on the platform she found herself praying that the train would come before Oliver or her mother caught up with her, because she could not face either of them ... He might come in the car, if they had guessed what she meant to do, or Constance might come, or both of them, and Andria knew she couldn't talk to them, she never wanted to see either of them again, ever ... they had betrayed her, both of them had betrayed her ...

"Oh Oliver," she thought in anguish. "How could you, how could you do such a thing? You knew I loved you ... "

The train came in, sliding to a halt, and Andria got in, sinking into a vacant seat and closing her eyes. Someone offered to put her suitcase on the rack, and she smiled briefly, then closed her eyes again, aware that the train was warm and heated and that she was safe from pursuit, at least temporarily, thank God.

Afterwards Andria could never remember anything about the journey clearly. She sat in a stupor of misery, her eyes closed, trying to block out the memory of those two, naked in bed together, her mother's hair falling over her bare shoulders and touching Oliver's head as it left the pillow ... and the look of guilt on both their faces ...

"She *knew* I loved him," Andria thought. "She knew, I told her . . . she can have any man she wants but she had to have Oliver . . ."

A flood of murderous hatred surged up in her, and she understood now how crimes of passion happen, and how the person must have felt — sick and shocked and totally disbelieving . . .

Outside the tube station the rain was pouring down, cold relentless sheets of it, and as the passengers came out of their temporary shelter most of them paused, grimaced, and put up their umbrellas. Andria came out slowly and began to walk, her feet soaked, water running out of her bedraggled hair, the suitcase in her icy left hand almost dragging along the pavement. Her skirt clung to her legs, but she walked grimly on, ploughing straight through the gathering puddles, until she came to a mews and turned wearily down it.

She stopped outside the flat door, fumbled for a moment in her bag, then pressed her thumb on the door bell, praying that Suky would be in. After a moment she heard footsteps coming downstairs, and Suky appeared in the doorway.

"Andy!" she exclaimed. "Come in, you — you're soaked!"

Andria smiled briefly and began to toil up the narrow stairs to the flat, still dragging the suitcase. Halfway up Suky took it from her, giving her a long searching look, and they went into the lounge together.

"You'd better get out of those wet clothes," Suky said, putting the suitcase down. "What happened? Did Oliver's car break down?"

"No," Andria shook her head. "Nothing like that . . ."

Her lips quivered, then suddenly, she sneezed, and Suky became the brisk efficient hospital nurse she was.

"Go and have a hot shower straight away," she said firmly. "Now, before you catch a terrible cold. I'll unpack your case for you. Go on."

Andria moved like a robot towards the tiny bathroom, and Suky picked up the suitcase and took it into the bedroom. As she tidied Andria's clothes away she wondered what had happened — Andria appeared to be in a state of shock, and Suky went into the kitchen to make tea for them both, ladling sugar liberally into Andria's mug.

A few minutes later Andria re-appeared, wearing a thick woollen dressing-gown, her hair swathed in a towel, and Suky turned with a quick smile.

"Sit down and have some tea," she said. "No, come on, you need it."

Andria took the mug and sipped obediently, staring straight ahead of her, her face set in an expression of misery, and Suky slipped an arm round her shoulders.

"Come on, love," she said gently. "What's wrong? Want to talk about it?"

Andria's lips quivered, and tears began to run down her white face.

"Oh, Suky, how could they do it, how *could* they?"

"How could they do what?" Suky asked, reaching for the tissue box and thrusting one into Andria's hand.

"My — my mother," Andria's voice was a husky whisper. "My mother and — and Oliver!"

"What?" Suky gasped, feeling as if someone had hit her in the stomach, and Andria struggled for a moment with her tears, then began to talk.

Suky sat listening, tight-lipped, while the whole sorry story poured out, and Andria clung to her hand like a small, hurt child.

"I dropped the tray," Andria said dully. "And then I ran . . . "

"Andy, you — you couldn't have been mistaken, could you?" Suky knew the words sounded puerile even as she said them. "I mean, they weren't just — just talking, were they?"

"With no clothes on and in bed?" Andria's smile was twisted.

"What happened then?" Suky asked.

"I packed my suitcase and left," Andria said, her voice flat with exhaustion. "Constance called out to me but I didn't take any notice. I walked to the station and caught the first train back to London."

"I don't know what to say," Suky shook her head, as if she still couldn't believe what she had heard.

"There's not much you can say," Andria ran her hand wearily across her eyes. "I thought Oliver loved me, and Constance knew I loved him, I never thought they — they'd . . . "

"Neither would any decent person," Suky said grimly, as Andria's tears flowed again. "To be honest, Andy, I always thought Oliver was rather an opportunist, but I never dreamed he was capable of that . . ."

"He used me," Andria whispered. "He used me to get to my mother."

"I think you're right," Suky said reluctantly. "Andy, you're well rid of him — I know you don't think so now, but you are."

"Am I well rid of my mother, too?" Andria asked bitterly, and Suky's lips tightened.

"I think you might quite well be," she said, and there was a long silence.

"I never want to see either of them again," Andria said, in a tone of total finality. "And I don't want any help from her, either — if she sends me any money I shall send it straight back."

Suky made no reply. What was there to say? In Andria's place she would have felt the same.

"Have some more tea," she said practically. "Then I think you ought to try and eat something."

"I don't think I could," Andria gave a small crooked smile. "Suky, you won't tell anyone about this, will you? I couldn't bear it if anyone else knew. You won't, will you?"

"No, you needn't worry about that," Suky promised quietly. If anyone wants to know I'll just say you broke off your engagement because you decided you weren't suited, something like that. OK?"

Andria nodded. It was as good an explanation as any, and at least there had been no one else in her mother's house to witness what had gone on.

"Oh, I nearly forgot," Suky exclaimed suddenly. "Horry phoned, something about a TV advertisement – can you ring him back, Andy? I know you probably don't feel like it," she said quickly, "but if you're going to be fully independent then you need all the work you can get."

Andria nodded, achieving a wan smile. Never had she felt less like work, but her common sense told her that Suky was right.

"I'll do it now," she said, getting up rather unsteadily. "Thanks, Suky."

She went to the phone, and Suky went

into the kitchen, thinking not for the first time that Andria was too sensitive for the profession she had chosen, if chosen was the right word. Andria had been born into it, she knew nothing else, and Suky, reaching for a basin and some eggs, shook her head again.

"Thank goodness I'm just *ordinary*," she muttered, listening to the quiet murmur of Andria's voice as she talked to her agent, Horry Bakewell. "I wonder if she *would* eat any of this?"

Andria ate a little of the omelette Suky put before her, gulping it as if she found it difficult to swallow. Finally she laid down her fork, smiled apologetically at her friend, and said:

"It was nice, Suky, but I'm not very hungry. Is it — is it still raining?"

"Bucketing down the last time I looked," Suky said. "Andy, will you be all right if I go out for a little while? I'm meeting Bill at three o'clock to look at a flat we thought we might buy. It isn't too expensive and Bill says it sounds all right, for the time being at least."

"Of course you must go," Andria said quickly. "You might lose it if you hang around and then I'd never forgive myself. I'll be all right, Suky. Horry doesn't want to see me and the TV thing isn't until tomorrow. I'll probably lie down for a bit — I've got a headache."

"To which you're quite entitled," Suky said drily.

They cleared away the remnants of the meal, Andria took two aspirins and went to lie down, and Suky got ready to meet her fiance. She was reluctant to leave Andria alone, but there didn't seem to be anything else she could do for her, and when she peeped into her bedroom just before she left she saw that Andria had fallen into an exhausted sleep, which Suky thought was probably the best thing for her.

Suky went quietly downstairs, wondering how much to say to Bill, and deciding to stick to the story she and Andria had decided to tell — the real truth seemed sordid and indecent . . .

"I wonder if Oliver will come crawling round here to try and patch it up?" Suky thought, as she walked to her rendezvous. "With Andy in her present mood he wouldn't stand much of a chance."

And Andria's mother, what was she

thinking at this present moment? Did she have any regrets, any feelings of remorse for the havoc she had caused in her daughter's life?

"Probably not," Suky thought, and then she caught sight of her fiancé, and hurried to meet him.

3

ANDRIA never knew how she got through the next few days. She did everything automatically, getting up, forcing down some breakfast to please Suky, going out to appointments, working with other actors and actresses. There seemed to be two Andrias — the one who carried on as if everything was entirely normal, and the one who ached inside . . .

She did the TV advertisement, rehearsed for the TV part, and brought home a script Horry gave her to read. It was a heavy melodrama, and she pulled a face as she scanned the first few pages. Suky, who was reading over her shoulder, suddenly choked and began to giggle, then apologised.

"I'm sorry," she said, her hazel eyes dancing. "But Andy, it's so miserable it's *funny!*"

A few pages later Andria decided Suky was right and went to phone Horry.

"Awful, is it, darling?" Horry said

sympathetically. "Thought it might be. All right, bring it back, I'll have a word with the writer, maybe he can do something about it."

"Well, at the moment it either makes you want to rush off and end it all, or it makes you roll around laughing," Andria said, listening to explosions of merriment coming from Suky. "I can't see anyone wanting to produce it as it is now."

"Any good as a farce?" her agent asked hopefully.

"It might be if he could lighten the gloom a bit," Andria said thoughtfully. "I'll bring it back tomorrow, shall I?"

"OK." Horry hung up, and Andria went back to Suky, who was still reading the script, tears of laughter running down her face.

"Oh, Andy, I don't know anyone who could act in this," she said, fishing out a handkerchief and mopping her streaming eyes. "Who did Horry say wrote it?"

"A young actor with literary aspirations," Andria smiled back. "You know how kind Horry is, he can't bear to discourage anyone . . . Are you meeting Bill today?"

"No, I'm working this afternoon," Suky sobered up. "We've decided on the flat, by the way. It needs some decorating but it isn't too awful. Very small kitchen but it will do for now."

"I'd like to see it sometime," Andria said.

"Would you really?" Suky looked eager. "All right, the next time Bill and I go you must come too, if you can. Lunch, Andy?"

"All right."

Andria was still struggling with total loss of appetite, but she managed to eat enough to satisfy Suky, mostly because she had a feeling that if she didn't Suky would come home with a large bottle of foul tasting tonic and stand over her while she swallowed it!

Suky produced salad and fruit, and they discussed Andria's part in the TV play.

"We'll have finished shooting it by the end of the week," Andria said, putting down the apple she had started half eaten. "I must let Horry know I'm looking for something else."

"Tell him tomorrow when you take the script back," Suky said, her lips twitching with remembered mirth. "I suppose — I suppose you haven't heard anything from anyone?"

"Not a word," Andria shook her head. "But then, I didn't really expect to."

"What about that man, the producer," Suky said suddenly. "What was his name, Ellard something? Didn't you say he seemed to like your performance?"

"Well, yes, I think he did. But it was — it was Oliver he was interested in, and if — if Constance is going to be in any of his productions, then *I* don't want to know."

"Don't blame you," Suky said. "It was just an idea, that's all."

Suky went out, and Andria trailed into the kitchen to do a little hand washing. She was listlessly dunking some tights when the phone rang, and she went to answer it, praying that it wouldn't be Oliver or her mother.

"Hello?" The voice sounded familiar, but she couldn't quite place it. "Is that Andria?"

"Yes," she frowned. "Who — who is that?"

"Ellard Ashton here. I've got a proposition

to put to you, Andria. May I come round and see you?"

"Yes, I — I suppose so," Andria said, rather blankly. "What-what is it?"

"We'll discuss it when I see you," he said. "I'll be there in about half an hour."

There was a click, and Andria was left with the receiver in her hand, staring at it. Not knowing whether to be pleased or dismayed, she went quickly back into the kitchen and finished the washing, then into the bedroom to tidy herself up. Whatever it was, she must not be at a disadvantage with someone like Ellard Ashton.

"I hope he doesn't want me to work with Oliver or Constance," she thought. "Because I just can't."

He was punctual, coming up the stairs and into the flat with all the assurance of a successful man. As they shook hands he shot her a quick glance, and a little frown gathered between his brows.

"Would you like some coffee?" she asked, and he nodded.

"This is a very pleasant little place you have here," he remarked. "You share it with a friend, don't you?"

"Yes, my friend Suky. She's a nurse.

50

Will you excuse me, Ellard, I won't be a minute."

When she returned with the coffee he was sitting, apparently quite at his ease, in an armchair, looking down at the mews outside.

"Do you take sugar?" she asked, and he shook his head.

"How busy are you at the moment, Andria?" he asked.

"Well, I've nearly finished with a TV play, about another week should see it done," Andria replied. "Horry hasn't found me anything yet but I expect he will, he's very good."

"Would you consider a part in a new play I'm producing shortly?" Ellard asked, and she realised that he was watching her closely. "It's a farce but rather a good one — witty and sharp rather than smutty and vulgar. I think you'd do very well as one of the daughters of the two main characters."

"Well, thank you very much for considering me, Ellard." Andria looked down at her hands, discovered that they were trembling, and clasped them tightly in her lap. "There — there's just one thing — would I — would I have to work with Oliver or my — or Constance? Because just at the moment — well, I don't think I could."

There was a long pause, while she waited for him to say "why not?" She found that she could not look at him, but she heard the little sound as he replaced his cup in the saucer, and discovered that she was holding her breath.

"I see," he said, and his tone was quite gentle. "Well, I won't ask why, but I think I can guess ... No, Andria, you won't have to see either of them, it's an entirely separate production at a different theatre, nothing to do with them. You need have no fears on that score, so what about it?"

"Thank you, Ellard," she said huskily, limp with sheer relief. "I'd like to try."

"Good." She looked across at him, and saw that he was smiling. "I'll send you the script, and you can tell your agent you're booked indefinitely. This is nice coffee, by the way. There wouldn't be another one going by any chance?"

She brought him another cup and a slice of a cake Suky had made, and they chatted for a while, mostly about the best way to play farce, agreeing that it was one of the most difficult things to get right.

"The whole thing tends to disintegrate into horse play if you're not very careful," Ellard said, and Andria nodded. "Rather like a pantomime."

"That was the first production I was in, a pantomime," Andria said, smiling. "I was six."

"I should imagine you were a beautiful child, too," Ellard remarked, so matter-of-factly that she didn't know whether it was intended for a compliment or not. "What did you do?"

"We all came out of a huge Christmas pudding," Andria told him, and he grinned. "It really didn't have anything to do with the story, but the audience liked it. We were dressed up as robins."

Ellard chuckled again, and Andria thought suddenly:

"He's not the least bit formidable, why was I so in awe of him?"

She had a sudden perverse impulse to ask how Oliver was getting on in his part, but changed her mind as quickly. Why should she care what Oliver was doing? He could be the world's biggest flop as far as she was concerned . . .

Ellard put down his plate with a sigh of repletion, and got up to go.

"Right," he said briskly. "I'll see you in about a week's time. And Andria, may I make a suggestion? Can you possibly become a little plumper? I don't care for hollow cheekbones, even with bone structure like yours."

"I'll try," she said, flushing a little, and he nodded gravely.

"Good girl," he said. "Thanks for the coffee, and tell Suky she's going to be a wonderful wife. Goodbye."

She went to the bottom of the stairs with him and watched him drive away, then slowly climbed back to the flat, feeling that something very important had happened. Working with Ellard could do her career nothing but good — if only her personal life was happier . . .

When Suky came back and heard the news she was delighted.

"Do you know, I'm not the least bit surprised, Andy?" she said. "Ellard probably liked that little scene you did opposite — "

She stopped, and Andria said, with composure:

"You don't have to stop using Oliver's name, Suky — I'll have to get a bit thicker-skinned where he's concerned."

"Good," Suky said bluntly. "Well, as I was saying, Ellard probably liked what you did and decided to offer you a part — do you know who you'll be working with?"

"Not yet," Andria shook her head. "But Ellard's sending me a script, so he may tell me then."

"Exciting, isn't it?" Suky grinned, and Andria had a sudden pang of conscience.

"You are a pet, Suky," she said, huskily. "I've been an absolute drip for weeks, and you haven't lost your temper with me once — thanks."

"What are friends for?" Suky asked, giving her a sort of cross between a slap and a pat. "And what about all the times I moaned to you about the exams and that *awful* Sister Donovan? You must have been sick of the sound of my voice."

"Not really, I was too sorry for you!"

They both laughed, and Andria offered to cook supper as a sign of penitence. Suky accepted gratefully, and eased off her shoes, and Andria wondered, not for the first time, how nurses managed to cope with all the hard work caring for the sick entailed.

Ellard was as good as his word. The script arrived the next morning, together with a letter telling her which part he wanted her to play. She read the whole play through several times, giggling at intervals, then read her own part more carefully. She was cast as Jemima, the youngest daughter of Sir Rhoderick and Lady Penhallow, and as she read she began to picture how she would play it — mischievous and perky or slightly malicious and pert?

"I expect Ellard will have his own ideas," she thought as she finally laid the script down. "But the timing is going to be very tricky — all those bedroom doors opening and shutting at just the right moment!" She caught herself yawning, and went into the kitchen to get a hot drink. As she had promised Ellard, she was eating a little more, and some of her lost colour had come back into her face. As Suky had gently said to her once, life — and the show — must go on . . .

Good resolutions notwithstanding, it was a nervous and pale Andria who turned up to rehearsals on the appointed day. She was admitted to the theatre by the doorman, and the first thing she heard as she walked down the central aisle of the theatre were voices raised in violent altercation.

"No, no, no!" Someone was saying, and Andria thought she recognised the voice. "No, Charlie, Julia *isn't* promiscuous, just a little — well — "

"Frisky?" Someone suggested, sounding as if they were smiling, and Andria looked up at the stage and saw that most of the cast were there already, although she wasn't late. She climbed quietly on to the stage, glancing round to see if she did know anyone, and realised that she was right about the voice. It belonged to Helen Gibson, one of the legends of the theatre, and Miss Gibson looked hot, mulish and flustered, which surprised Andria.

"Helen darling, calm down," Ellard said, from his chair at the side of the stage. "You're quite right, of course, but let's keep our cool, shall we? Charlie, you don't *know* your wife invited her old boy-friend to stay, you only suspect, so don't come on quite so strong, eh?"

Helen nodded, gave a long sigh, then suddenly caught sight of Andria and stared at her for an uncomfortable moment. Then, unexpectedly, her famous smile flashed out.

"You were right, Ellard," she said. "She's lovelier even than her mother . . . Come here, child."

Andria obeyed, eyes enormous with fright, and Helen kissed her.

"Don't look so scared," she said. "No one's going to eat you."

"I wouldn't mind," Charlie said, *sotto voce*, and Andria had to suppress a sudden giggle.

Ellard introduced her to the rest of the cast, and Andria, that hurdle over, sat down and watched while Helen and Charlie Dawson played the rest of their scene.

"They're really *smooth*," Andria thought, and then it was her turn, an amusing little scene with the girl who was playing her sister, Emily.

Emily's part was taken by a comparative newcomer, a pretty blonde girl called Yvonne Lake, and Andria found her very easy to work with. She was surprised when Ellard announced that they would break for lunch, and as she left the theatre Yvonne touched her arm and suggested a sandwich in the nearest convenient cafe.

"I'm absolutely starving," she confessed, as they fell into step along the pavement. "I was so nervous I couldn't eat any breakfast – I'd have been sick. You're pretty good, aren't you? But then you should be – Constance Vincent is your mother, isn't she?"

"Yes, she is," Andria kept her tone light. "And you're good too, Yvonne.

"I hope so," Yvonne said, pushing the cafe door open. "I don't come from a theatrical family and my parents didn't really want me to be an actress. But, here I am."

"Good for you," Andria said. "How about that table over there? The one in the corner."

"What do you think of the rest of the cast?" Yvonne asked, as they sat down. "I like Helen but I'm scared stiff of her. You've got to watch Charlie though, he's a bit of a wolf."

"Thanks for the warning, I'll watch out

for him. I like your opposite number, what's his name, Kenneth?"

"Kenneth Adams. Yes, he is nice, but I'm not so sure about yours, Andria. He's got a — a *waspish* sort of a tongue for such a young guy, and — " Yvonne hesitated, coloured a little, then continued — "and he seems to have an uncanny knack of discovering things you'd rather people *didn't* know, if you take my meaning."

"I'll be careful," Andria said, and just then the waiter came up to take their order.

To her surprise she found she was hungry, and as they attacked their sandwiches she considered what Yvonne had said about Andria's opposite number, Nigel Timmings. Yvonne might be right, she thought, remembering the disconcertingly sharp gaze Nigel had directed at her. Normally she would have simply shrugged and ignored that sort of thing, but in her present sensitive state she could definitely do without it.

"This coffee isn't bad, is it?" Yvonne commented, as she put down her cup. "Fancy another one?"

"Yes, I think I would. Then I suppose

we'd better get back."

"M'm, Ellard's a terror for proper time keeping. But I like him, don't you?"

"Yes, I do. It must be very hard work keeping three theatres on the go and everything properly done."

"I should say so," Yvonne nodded. "And he's young too, isn't he?"

She eyed Andria thoughtfully for a moment, then asked: "Have you got a — a regular boy-friend, Andria?"

"I-I did have, but we — split up." Andria should have been prepared for the question, but she couldn't help a tiny wince. "We weren't really suited."

"Well, better to find out now than after you were married or got pregnant or something," Yvonne said philosophically. "I haven't, because I decided to concentrate on my career for the time being. I could go for Kenneth, though."

Andria laughed, and a few minutes later they were walking back to the theatre.

The afternoon was a continuation of the morning. Ellard took them through the play quickly, explaining roughly how he thought each scene should be played, and Andria sat listening, beginning to see why Ellard had been so successful. He seemed intuitive and intelligent, and very considerate of his actors, but at the same time Andria had the feeling that he would stand no nonsense. However, he seemed not to mind constructive suggestions, and one by one all the actors made them, except Nigel, who sat quietly watching everyone else, a little smile playing around his lips.

"Yvonne could be right," Andria thought, as she stood up to do the scene where her stage father caught her in a compromising situation with her boy-friend. "He looks vaguely like a — a *cat.*"

"What's the meaning of this?" Charlie thundered, in his character of Sir Rhoderick. "Well, speak, boy, don't just stand there!"

Nigel spluttered helplessly as the script demanded, Andria cowered behind him, and Helen swept on to the stage and, as Yvonne said later, laid about her . . .

"Good, it's coming along very well," Ellard said, gathering up his script. "Tomorrow, then, at ten o'clock? Charlie, about the . . . "

The actors straggled out of the theatre, and to Andria's surprise Nigel joined her, winding an immensely long red scarf round his neck.

"I think you're going my way," he said. "You live in Conway Mews, don't you? I usually walk home, saves paying for a taxi. My car's in for a check up."

"I haven't got a car," Andria smiled. If Nigel wanted to make a friendly gesture, well, fine . . . "My room mate Suky has, though. She's a nurse."

"Ugh!" Nigel shuddered. "I *loathe* hospitals, they smell so . . . "

"Well, I suppose it's a *good* smell," Andria pointed out. "Think of all that disinfectant killing all those germs."

"That's one way of looking at it," Nigel admitted. "I'm surprised you don't have a car, though. Was it the problem of garaging?"

"Partly." They paused on the edge of the pavement, waiting for a break in the traffic before they crossed the road. "We do rent a garage under the flat, but Suky's car was more important. Quick, Nigel . . . "

They arrived on the other side of the road, panting a little.

"It gets worse, not better," Nigel commented. "We turn down here, don't we? By the way, what do you think of the play, Andria? I think it's quite clever, myself."

"I think so, too." Faintly surprised by what he had said, Andria nodded. She would have expected a more caustic remark, somehow. Possibly she had misjudged Nigel. "It must be very difficult to write effective farce."

"Fiendishly," Nigel gave his scarf a tweak as a coil of it threatened to trail along the ground. "What do you think of the cast?"

"I think we're working well together," Andria said. "I thought Helen would be formidable, but she isn't, is she?"

"We haven't seen her in one of her famous rages yet," Nigel pointed out, with a little crooked smile. "Does your mother get into states like that, Andria?"

"Not often," Andria replied, cautiously. "Would you like a coffee, Nigel? Or do you have other plans for the evening?"

"Thanks, sweetie, but my girl-friend has something fabulous planned for tonight, gastronomically speaking," Nigel said, tweaking at his scarf again. "See you in the morning. Bye."

He went, and Andria drew a ragged

breath. She would have to learn to quell that shaking feeling inside her every time her mother's name was mentioned, because mentioned it would be, she couldn't escape that fact . . .

Suky was at home, working in the kitchen, but she looked up with a smile as Andria came in.

"How did it go?" she asked, reaching for a carrot.

"Fine, much better than I thought it would," Andria put her handbag down. "I'll just wash my hands, then I'll come and help you."

Suky listened with genuine interest as Andria outlined her day, then gave a sigh.

"Makes my work seem positively humdrum," she said, brushing a strand of soft blonde hair out of her eyes. "By the way, Andy, I'm sorry but I'm going to be on nights for the next few weeks."

"Oh, Suky!" Andria exclaimed sympathetically. "That's a pain, isn't it?"

"Somebody has to do it," Suky said matter-of-factly.

"Well, at least you can sleep during the day in peace, I shan't be in to disturb you," Andria said. "Have you got Sundays off?"

"Yes, thank goodness," Suky grinned. "At least I can see Bill then . . . can you go and set the table?"

Andria departed, forcing away a wave of depression which threatened to engulf her. How trivial her own profession seemed compared to Suky's! She had said this to her friend once, and Suky had pointed out that Andria probably gave pleasure to thousands of people, and what was trivial about that?

The next few days seemed composed of work, hard work and nothing but work, but the play began to come alive, and Ellard was obviously very pleased. He took the whole cast out to dinner one evening, and as Andria looked across the table at him, relaxed and smiling, he seemed to be a different person from the disciplined and forceful character who corrected, coerced and guided them during the day.

"I think it's going to be splendid, Ellard," Helen said, beaming round the table, and Nigel, who was sitting beside Andria, murmured:

"Her Majesty has spoken . . . "

"I think she could be right," Kenneth

said from his other side. "It's got a good feel about it, somehow."

"Have you ever been in a flop, Andy?" Nigel asked, and she shook her head.

"Not a flop exactly," she replied. "But I was in a play which only ran for four weeks once. It was a pity because it was a good play. I felt sorry for the author."

"Yes, you're a kindly wee soul, aren't you?" Kenneth said, and she glanced sideways at him as she detected for the first time the very faintest hint of a Scots accent.

"Aberdeen," he said, as if he had read her thoughts. "I've been trying to get rid of the accent for years."

"Then don't," Andria smiled back at him. "It's nice."

Their coffee appeared, and shortly afterwards the party broke up, and Andria and Nigel shared a taxi home.

"Will your mother be gracing our opening night with her presence?" Nigel asked, as the taxi moved off.

"I — I don't know," Andria stammered, caught off guard. "She — she's pretty busy herself at the moment."

Nigel said no more, but the curiously

cat-like little smile she had noticed once before played for an instant round his lips, and she felt an uneasy qualm. Then she told herself not to be stupid — what did it matter what Nigel thought or didn't think? It was nothing to do with him, anyway . . .

"That was a terrific dinner Ellard treated us to tonight," she said, changing the subject. "Why is it that everything tastes better when you eat out even if you could cook it just as well yourself?"

"I've often wondered that myself," Nigel said. "I suppose with Ellard's money he can afford to eat well."

"Suppose so," Andria agreed.

She looked out of the window at the lights of London, and a wave of sheer affection for the place swept through her.

"Where is your mother playing now, Andy?" Nigel asked, his tone casual, and she turned her head just a fraction too sharply.

"M — Manchester, in another one of Ellard's plays," she said, wishing Nigel would get off the subject of her mother. "I met the playwright a few weeks ago. His name is Michael Lester. It's a thriller but an unusual one."

"Ah," Nigel said, nodding. "Ellard certainly gathers the talent about him, doesn't he?"

"M'm." Andria nodded. "He does."

The taxi driver took her to the top of the mews, and waited until she was safely inside the flat. As she climbed the stairs Andria wondered uneasily if somehow or other rumours about what had happened were circulating around on the grape vine every profession or trade has, though nobody could know the details unless Constance or Oliver told them, and Andria felt sure neither of them would do *that*.

The flat felt curiously empty without Suky, and Andria undressed slowly, wondering what problems her friend had been called upon to deal with that night.

The next morning she got up quietly, creeping around so as not to disturb Suky, who was asleep. She must have come in equally quietly a little earlier and gone straight to bed. Andria left the flat and walked to the theatre, revelling in the warm sunshine, and thinking that perhaps this was spring at last. It had certainly taken its time arriving.

She went into the theatre and found the others already there, including Ellard, who was talking quietly to Yvonne and Kenneth. Nigel was sitting on an upturned wooden box, reading a newspaper, and he looked up with a smile.

"Hey, just the person I've been waiting for," he said. "Have you seen the paper this morning, Andy?"

He handed it to her, jabbing a long forefinger at the page, and she looked at it, puzzled.

It was a photograph, a little blurred and out of focus as if the photographer had been in a hurry, but she had no difficulty in recognising the subjects. Smiling broadly, the faces of her mother and Oliver leaped out of the page at her.

"Famous actress engaged," said the caption. "Constance Vincent with her fiancé, Oliver Prentiss. Miss Vincent said . . . "

4

THE newspaper fell out of her nerveless fingers, and a wave of sick giddiness engulfed her. She swayed, dimly aware that people were moving towards her, and that someone had seized her elbow in a hard steadying grip.

"All right, Andy, hold on to me." The voice seemed vaguely familiar, but she was totally incapable of holding on to anyone — all the strength seemed to have drained from her limbs, and the owner of the voice steered her into a chair, pushed her head between her knees, and held it there with a firm hand.

She stared at the floor, still struggling with nausea, listening dazedly to the voices talking around her.

"Shouldn't she have some brandy?"

"No, tea with sugar — I'll get it."

"I — I'll be all right," she croaked through her dry mouth. "S — sorry . . ."

"No, sit still." She realised that it was Ellard she was half leaning against,

71

and suddenly embarrassed, she struggled upright and stared round her, breathing hard.

"God, Andy, you look awful," Kenneth blurted, with Scots bluntness. "Did you know about your mother? Nigel, you little sh — you little worm . . . "

"For heaven's sake, how was I to know?" Nigel had the grace to look slightly confused. "I thought she'd like to see the photo."

"Well, she's seen it now," Charlie said acidly. "Helen, I think Andy should lie down for a few minutes.

"Yes, of course." Helen moved over and helped Andria to her feet. "We'll be in my dressing-room."

Andria went with her, her knees still trembling with weakness, and Helen steered her on to the settee and stood for a moment, looking down at her.

"Sorry to make such a scene," Andria's voice shook. "It — it gave me such a shock . . . "

"That much was apparent," Helen said, then looked away as a hesitant knock came at the door.

"Come in," she called, and Yvonne appeared, carrying a steaming mug.

"Are you feeling OK now, Andy?" she asked, looking very concerned, and Andria nodded.

Yvonne handed her the mug carefully, smiled nervously at Helen, and almost backed out of the dressing-room, closing the door quietly behind her.

"A nice child, that," Helen commented. "Try and drink that, Andy, even if it does taste like liquid syrup."

Andria sipped obediently, and slowly the walls of the small room took firm shape, and Helen's classically lovely face stopped blurring and came into proper focus.

Helen sat down on her dressing-table stool and smiled at Andria, who achieved a faint, lopsided smile in return.

"Now that wasn't just because your mother had got engaged, was it, child?" Helen asked gently. "Want to talk or would you rather not?"

It was easier than Andria had imagined, and Helen listened, a frown gathering between her fine eyebrows, but she did not interrupt.

"I — I thought it would just be one of Con's affairs," Andria faltered. "I never thought — I mean, she's nine years older than he is, for a start . . . "

"Which is about the same difference there is between him and you," Helen pointed out gently. "It could work, Andy — not that I approve of the way they've gone about things, it was insensitive to say the least. To be truthful with you, I've never liked your mother, though she is a brilliant actress, of course. You say you haven't heard from her since?"

"No," Andria shook her head. "And I don't want to."

"I don't blame you," Helen said. "Tell me, that business of Nigel showing you the newspaper — did he know it would upset you?"

"I think he guessed we'd had a row or something," Andria said. "He was asking me some funny little questions."

"That boy has the soul of a gossip columnist," Helen said acidly. "A pity, he has the makings of a very fine actor. I might get Charlie to have a word with him, quietly of course."

Andria could imagine what Charlie's idea of a quiet word would be, and a reluctant grin appeared on her face.

"*That's* better," Helen exclaimed. "Now

74

if you've swallowed that stuff, shall we get back to work? Or would you rather stay here for a bit?"

"No, I'll come," Andria stood up slowly, relieved to find that this time her legs would support her. "We've wasted enough time already."

"Good," Helen nodded approval. "Come along, then. And Andria, for what it's worth, I think your Oliver may have made the biggest mistake of his life in leaving you."

They returned to the stage, and as Andria quietly reseated herself Ellard gave her a quick, reassuring smile, then went on with what he was saying as if nothing had happened. No one made any reference to it, but all through the day Andria was conscious of their unspoken sympathy, and even Nigel curbed his sharp tongue and concentrated on his part. There was a faintly chastened air about him, and she wondered if during her absence the others had given him an unpalatable piece of their minds . . .

As they were gathering up their belongings to leave that evening, Ellard touched her arm gently.

"If you're not doing anything tonight, Andy, come and eat with me," he said, smiling. "There's no need to go home and change, I know a quiet little place no one dresses up for, and frankly, I'm starving."

"Thanks, I — I'd like to," Andria smiled back. "If you don't mind taking me like this."

"You look fine. Goodnight, everyone, be on time in the morning." Ellard looked round at his cast. "It's going well, I'm very pleased."

Andria went with him to where he had parked his car, shivering a little in the cooler night air, almost wishing she had refused Ellard's invitation. She felt suddenly drained, physically and emotionally, and she almost crawled into the passenger seat.

"Tired?" Ellard fastened his seat belt. "What you need is food. Sorry to sound callous, but you do."

"You may be right," Andria admitted. "Ellard, I hope — I hope this morning didn't disrupt anything too much."

"Only for a disgusted few minutes," Ellard whipped the car deftly round a corner.

"Disgust at Constance, of course — I think everyone knows roughly what happened, Andy, but it will go no further, not from them, not even from Nigel."

"Thank you."

"All right. Now let's try and forget it, shall we? What do you fancy? Steak? You look as if you could do with a large juicy one."

"Why not?" Andria sat upright. "With all the trimmings?"

"With *everything*," Ellard grinned.

His hand covered hers for a moment, then was withdrawn to regrip the driving wheel.

Ellard was right about the restaurant. It was quiet and intimate, no one was dressed up, and she relaxed in her chair with a sigh. The waiter passed her the menu and she glanced down it, stifling a sudden yawn, hoping Ellard hadn't noticed it. He was studying the menu, so perhaps he hadn't . . .

He enquired if she still wanted steak, and she nodded.

Ellard ordered for them both, including a bottle of red wine, then rested his elbows on the table and smiled across at Andria.

"How's your nurse friend coping with night duty?" he asked.

"Not too badly, I think. I don't see much of her now, because when I'm in she's out. It's the first few days she finds difficult to adjust to."

"I don't think I'd ever adjust," Ellard said frankly. "Tell me, Andria, what do you think of the play? Will it be a success?"

"With Helen and Charlie and you directing it? Of course it will."

"Aha, a vote of confidence from my best young actress," Ellard grinned. "I think it will too . . ."

"How — how is the other play coming along?" Andria had to force herself to ask. "The one with — with — the one Oliver is in."

"Very well, according to my stage manager," Ellard said, his voice as deliberately calm as hers had been. "We shall have two successes on our hands at round about the same time."

"M'm. Ellard, would you mind if I ask you something? I've always wanted to know how you've been so successful in such a short space of time. I mean, you — you're not very old, are you, to be in control of so many projects all at the same time. I have wondered how it happened."

"Hard work and a great deal of luck," Ellard said. "I started off in a rather sleazy little place in New York and the first production took off — there was even a film. After that I didn't look back."

"What were you doing in New York?" she asked. "You're English, aren't you?"

There was a pause, and then Ellard said:

"I was following my fiancée, hoping to persuade her to come back to me. I didn't succeed but I did meet this extremely talented young playwright who'd managed to get hold of a rundown theatre, and we teamed up. We still work together when I'm in New York. His name is Anthony Segall, you may have heard of him."

"I think I have," Andria frowned, trying to remember. "Didn't he write 'Player's Way'?"

"Yes, he did."

The waiter came with their first course, and as she picked up her knife and fork Andria suddenly wondered why Ellard's fiancée had left him, and how upset he had been. He had mentioned it calmly enough, and it had obviously been some time ago, but she hesitated before returning to the subject.

"Was — was your fiancée an actress?" she asked, and Ellard nodded.

"We were both very young," he said quietly. "And we were going to set the world alight — together, of course . . . then quite by chance she met this film producer, he offered her a part, I wasn't included, and off she went. It happens."

There was no trace of bitterness in his voice, but she felt a pang of sympathy for him nevertheless. He must have been terribly hurt, but he had bounced back with courage and resource.

"Did she — was she a success?"

"She was." He filled both their glasses. "She's a big star now, married to the producer, who's twice her age and has the sense to look the other way upon occasions. That's not spite, Andy, it's a statement of fact. How's the steak?"

"Fine." She took another bite. "Ellard, did — did whatever happened to you — well, did it make you . . . " her voice trailed off, and Ellard gave an amused little smile.

"Distrust women? No, of course not, not when I got over it, at any rate. Looking back, I can't really blame Sheila, it was such a tempting offer and we'd had no real luck for over a year."

"I sometimes wonder why we do it," Andria said suddenly. "All the stress and heartbreak . . . "

"Because it's in our blood," Ellard smiled. "Because we can't help it, and you know that's so, Andy."

"I suppose it is," she acknowledged. "But it's very hard sometimes."

"Any job is," Ellard pointed out. "More salad?"

She shook her head, wishing she could ask him more about his lost love, and deciding that she couldn't. She was begining to relax, and Ellard started talking about a novel he had recently read which he thought would make a good stage play. She listened, making the odd comment here and there, and wishing she felt more wide awake and lively. The shock of finding out about her mother and Oliver seemed to have dulled her wits and exhausted her.

" . . . scene two would be difficult," Ellard was saying. "I don't know yet how

81

it could be tackled — any ideas, Andy?"

She struggled to gather her depleted forces.

"Would it be possible to black out half the stage?"

"It might," Ellard turned the glass thoughtfully in his fingers. Long, sensitive fingers, like a musician or a surgeon, she thought. "It's an idea, Andy."

He smiled across at her, hesitated, then asked:

"If it isn't an impertinent question, Andy, who *was* your father? Was he an actor?"

"No, he was a musician, a violinist. He died before I was born so I never knew him. It was TB. Nobody seemed to realise he'd got it until it was too late."

"Bad luck," Ellard commented. "So Constance brought you up on her own?"

"If dumping me on a succession of baby minders could be called that, yes," Andria said, a tinge of bitterness in her voice. "No, Ellard, that *isn't* fair — she didn't have any close relatives, and she had to keep us both. She didn't have any choice but to leave me and get on with her career."

82

"Which she did admirably," Ellard commented.

"Yes," Andria nodded.

"You must have got those blue eyes from your father," Ellard said, turning his glass again. "And your hair from Constance — congratulations on picking the best from both parents."

Andria laughed, and Ellard's dark eyes crinkled at the corners in reply.

"You'll do fine, Andy," he said. "Helen thinks — and so do I — that you'll be an even better actress than Con, you're more sensitive to other people. Would you like some coffee?"

"I'd love some. Goodness, Ellard, is it eleven o'clock already?"

"M'm. We'd better go after this if we're to be at our brilliant best tomorrow."

She almost fell asleep in the car on the way back to the flat, and Ellard shook her gently awake, giving a little chuckle.

"Oh, I'm sorry," she said contritely. "I haven't been exactly dazzling company, have I?"

"You've been all right," Ellard got out of the car with her. "See you in the morning. Goodnight, Andy."

"Thank you for being so — so nice," she said, and in the dim light of a street lamp she thought his face altered in some indefinable way. "I did enjoy it, Ellard."

"So did I." He bent, and his lips brushed her cheek lightly. "I'll just see you safely through your front door."

She went slowly up the stairs, yawning almost uncontrollably, wriggled out of her clothes and almost fell into bed. She was asleep almost as soon as her head hit the pillow.

The next morning Andria discovered that Suky hadn't gone straight to bed, but was moving around in the kitchen, apparently getting breakfast for Andria and supper for herself.

"I'm beginning to adjust to the change of hours," she said, when Andria inquired what was happening. "Has anything interesting happened to you?"

She listened, frowning, while Andria told her about Constance and Oliver, then shook her head.

"I can't see that lasting for any length of time," she said bluntly. "There's too much of an age difference. I think so, anyway . . . So you went to dinner with Ellard?"

"Yes, and I could scarcely keep awake, I felt awful," Andria took a slice of toast from the rack and buttered it slowly. "He was so — so *nice*, Suky — they all were."

"I suppose," Suky said diffidently, rubbing her nose in the little gesture she used when she was embarrassed. "I suppose he hasn't fallen for you, has he, Andy?"

Andria's mouth fell open, and she stared at her friend in astonishment.

"I — I don't think so," she said eventually. "He was just being kind."

"Only a thought," Suky said, but her lips twitched at the corners in a knowing little smile. "He isn't dating anyone else at the moment, is he?"

"I don't think so, I'd have heard if he was."

"Aha," said Suky, and took a bite of her bacon. "Well, then."

"Well then what?" Andria retorted. "If you'd have seen the chaste little peck he gave me when we parted . . . "

"Maybe he's lulling you into a false sense of security," Suky giggled, and Andria giggled, too.

"Maybe," she agreed, and reached for the marmalade. "It's nice to see you *awake*, Suky."

Andria quickly dismissed Suky's remarks from her mind, and when she reached the theatre that morning there was certainly nothing in Ellard's manner to indicate that he had romantic feelings for Andria. His manner was friendly but brisk, and as Andy walked in he seemed to be settling an altercation between Helen and Charlie.

"Nonsense, Charlie, you're behaving like an amateur," Helen said acidly. "There's nothing wrong with Fred Higgins as your understudy — I'm surprised Ellard hasn't sorted that out before. He's a perfectly competent actor and you know it."

"I don't know anything of the sort," Charlie retorted. "And what a name — Fred Higgins! You'd have thought he'd have had the decency to change it, wouldn't you? But, of course, if Ellard thinks fit to use him, who am I to interfere?"

He stalked back to his chair and sat down, fuming, and Andria and Yvonne exchanged amused glances.

"Thank you, Charlie," Ellard said

gravely. "Of course I hope we won't have to use the understudies, any of them . . . Now shall we get on?"

"Awful, all that temper first thing in the morning," Nigel murmured. "I wonder he's got the energy . . . "

Fortunately Charlie soon recovered his composure and rehearsals continued without interruption. The play was beginning to come together well, and Helen remarked over their lunch-time sandwiches that she was sure they would have a hit.

"It will probably run for a year, if not longer," she predicted. "What do you think, Charlie?"

"Longer," Charlie said, and Andria was inclined to agree with him.

Several days went by, and she was beginning to recover from the shock of her mother and Oliver's engagement. Ellard didn't ask her out again, but Nigel, to her surprise, asked her round to have dinner with himself and his girl-friend. She accepted, and spent an enjoyable few hours. Nigel's girl-friend was a quiet, friendly girl called Annie, and it was obvious that they were extremely fond of each other.

"No, I'm not an actress, I work in a florist's," she said, in answer to Andria's question. "I think one actor in the family is enough, don't you?"

It was then that Andria saw the engagement ring on her finger, and demanded to know why Nigel hadn't told everyone.

"Because I want to keep her to myself, that's why," Nigel said calmly. "Well away from that lot we work with . . . Annie, darling, that smells heavenly . . . "

Andria discovered that the flat was Annie's, left to her by her mother, and that she and Nigel intended to get married quietly later that year.

"In between theatre activities," Nigel said, his mouth full of chicken. "We might even squeeze in a long weekend."

He smiled at Annie, and it was quite different from his normal faintly mocking little half grin. This smile was full of affection and tenderness, and Andria suddenly warmed to him. So Nigel was capable of loving someone — she had wondered . . .

"You must come and have a meal with me sometime," she said, as she and Annie washed up together in the kitchen. "I'd love to cook something for you, though I don't think it would be as good as that, Annie."

"I love cooking," Annie said. "It's one of my hobbies."

"The other one is needlework," Nigel said, appearing suddenly in the kitchen doorway. "You must show Andy some of the things you've made, darling, I feel quite proud of them myself."

"You didn't knit that long scarf for Nigel, by any chance?" Andria asked, and Annie nodded, giggling.

"I thought he was never going to let me stop," she said. "It looked like a boa constrictor in the end . . . there, that's done, let's go and sit down, shall we?"

They chatted for some time, then Nigel insisted that Andria must have a taxi home, and rang for one.

"It's safer," he said. "Annie got mugged once on the way home, which taught us both a lesson. See you in the morning, Andy."

She thanked them for a lovely evening, got into the taxi, and relaxed for a few minutes against the cushions, still feeling surprised at Nigel. Ellard had remarked during rehearsals that he was never astonished at people or what they did, evidently he had been right. Perhaps quiet, pretty Annie with her trusting brown eyes was exactly right for Nigel, and he for her . . .

As she went quickly down the mews, key in hand, she saw that the light was on in the lounge upstairs, and stopped, wondering who was there. Had Suky been taken ill, or had she taken the day off and come home?

She opened the door and called upstairs, and after a moment a light appeared on the landing and someone appeared, but it wasn't Suky. Andria stared up incredulously, and Oliver looked down at her, a half apologetic, half uneasy smile on his face.

For a moment she was too taken aback to speak, then she demanded, in a furious voice:

"How the — *how* did you get in?"

"I've still got the key you gave me, remember?" Oliver said, standing aside as she ran up the stairs. "Sorry if I startled you, but I didn't think you'd talk if I phoned, and I must speak to you, Andy."

"There's nothing to say." Andria walked into the lounge, then turned and faced him. "Please go away, Oliver, and you can leave that key, if you don't mind."

"I can't blame you for being bitter," Oliver said, laying the key on the coffee table. "But please listen for a few minutes, Andy, then I'll go."

"Since I can scarcely remove you physically, all right. You've got five minutes." She looked at her watch, her mouth a hard, tight line. "What is it?"

Oliver ran his hand through his thick hair in a gesture she remembered only too well, hesitated, then said:

"First of all, I want you to understand that what happened between Constance and me — well, it wasn't planned or anything like that — what I mean is, I didn't go there with the intention of seducing her. It wasn't *premeditated.*"

"That makes it better, I suppose." Andria's voice was venomously sarcastic, and Oliver winced. "All right. What was the next thing you wanted to say?"

"I — Con was very upset when you sent

the cheque back, Andy. She — she's afraid you won't be able to manage."

"I'll manage just fine," Andria's voice was grim. "I don't want her money."

"I can understand that." Oliver shifted uneasily from foot to foot, but Andria had no intention of asking him to sit down. "The other thing is this . . . "

He stopped, hesitated, then spoke in a rush of words.

"Andy, I know we've hurt you horribly, and I'm more sorry than I can say, but as soon as I saw Con — well, that was it as far as I'm concerned, and, well, I'm sorry . . . But the point is, Con's really upset, she'd do anything to make it up with you, and we wondered — we thought — would you come to our wedding? It would mean so much to her, to both of us if we felt you'd forgiven us."

"What!" Andria gasped, and Oliver went on, not giving her time to answer.

"She does — she does care for you, Andy, and so do I, and there's the other side of it, too. What are the Press going to make of it if you're not there? There are rumours flying around already, in fact. We've had reporters hanging about, I'm surprised if you haven't. It would be pretty embarrassing if they got hold of the real truth."

"They won't get it from me," Andria said, through clenched teeth. "Just keep your mouth shut, Oliver, you can do that, can't you? I certainly have no intention of turning up at your wedding just so that you can feel comfortable about what you did."

"There's no way we'd ever feel that," Oliver said quietly. "Please, Andy, change your mind — the wedding is in three weeks time. Con will send you an invite."

"Tell her not to bother," Andria said. "I have absolutely no intention of turning up."

Oliver looked searchingly at her set, angry face, gave a little shrug, said: "Well, I tried," and walked out of the room.

Andria stood listening until his footsteps faded into the distance, then sank down on the nearest chair, feeling angrier than she had ever felt in her life before. What did they think she was made of, wood? Didn't they realise what she had suffered? Or did they believe she was enough of a martyr to want to twist the knife in the wound? If so, they could think again . . . and if the Press did scent a story, Constance had dealt with troublesome reporters before, she was famous for it.

"They can go to hell for all I care," Andria muttered, and went wearily to bed.

5

SHE awoke the next morning totally unrefreshed, and pulled a face at herself in the mirror. Her eyes were heavy and dark-rimmed, she was pale, and she felt unhappy and listless. Suky had not arrived home, so there was no one to talk to over the cup of tea and slice of toast she played with for breakfast, and as she started out for the theatre she asked herself why she was going there at all.

"It's all pointless and artificial," she muttered as she went slowly downstairs. "I'd be more useful scrubbing floors or typing."

As if to match her sombre mood, the day was cool and cloudy, with a hint of rain in the air, and just as she reached the door of the theatre it began to pour in good earnest, and she hurried inside, wishing she had had the sense to bring an umbrella with her.

Most of the cast were already on stage, together with the understudies Ellard had decided on recently, and rehearsals began at once. Andria made a determined effort to concentrate, but her despondent mood must have been noticed, at least by Yvonne, because when they broke for coffee she asked if anything was the matter.

"Oliver came to see me last night," Andria said quietly, and Yvonne's mouth fell open. "He wants me to go to their wedding — his and Con's."

"Well of all — " Yvonne looked round, lowered her voice, and went on: "You won't go, will you?"

"No, of course not," Andria forced a smile. "All they want is to feel happy about what happened."

Yvonne snorted, loudly enough to make Kenneth, who was discussing something with Ellard, look sharply round at them. Andria gave Yvonne a warning look and she subsided, but Andria knew that she would probably tell Kenneth later, as they were becoming very good friends.

Lunch-time came, and Andria, who had forgotten to bring sandwiches, shared with Yvonne and Nigel, who had a large chunk of home-made cake with him, supplied of course by Annie, who had been experimenting in the kitchen again.

"It's lovely," Andria somehow achieved a smile. "It looks as if it would melt in the mouth."

"It'd do better melting inside you," Kenneth said forthrightly. "You're a bag of bones, girl."

Nigel looked critically at her.

"Yes, she is," he agreed, head on one side. "But what gorgeous bones they are!"

Everyone laughed, and even Andria managed a real smile.

"Thank you, Nigel," she said demurely. "That's a remark I shall always treasure."

"I aim to please," Nigel bowed gravely, but his eyes were knowing, and she was relieved when Ellard called them to order and afternoon rehearsals started.

Andria had not expected Ellard to draw her aside that evening when they had finished, but as she came out of the tiny dressing-room she shared with Yvonne he took her by the elbow.

"There's something wrong, isn't there?" he asked very quietly. "Are you doing anything tonight?"

"No," she shook her head. "Not really."

"Come to dinner with me."

"That's very kind of you, Ellard, but . . ."

"That's an order from the boss, so no buts," Ellard said, smiling. "You look ready to drop. Come along."

He almost marched her out to his car, calling out a cheerful goodnight to the others as he passed them. Andria got into the car, wondering if she could get through the evening without disgracing herself by crying, but unable to think of a convincing reason why she should be taken straight home.

"Where are we going?" she asked, and Ellard hesitated.

"If I got us some common old fish and chips, would you like to eat them at my place?" he asked.

"I — I'd love to," Andria said, surprised. "I like common old fish and chips."

"So do I. It's what I miss most when I'm in the US. Plaice or cod?"

"I don't mind. Thanks, Ellard."

She waited in the car while he hurried into the nearest fish and chip shop, returning triumphantly with several bulging paper parcels, which he stowed carefully on the back seat of the car.

"Right," he said, grinning. "Home we go."

Ellard's flat was smaller than Andria had thought it would be, but it was larger than the one she shared with Suky, and it had a modern, very well-fitted kitchen. She put the food on plates to keep hot while Ellard set the table in the lounge.

"Of course," he said as they sat down. "The proper way to eat this is out of newspaper with your fingers."

"Soused with vinegar," Andria said, smiling. "I like your furniture, Ellard."

"Do you? It's a motley collection, I'm afraid. I picked up a lot of it from antique shops, but that little bureau over there is the best of the collection. It's Sheraton."

"I thought it might be." She was beginning to feel better, and Ellard watched as the colour began to return to her face. "Those armchairs are rather nice, too."

"I had those re-upholstered. They were in an awful state when I got them. Fish OK?"

"M'm." Mouth full, she nodded. "Super. This really is nice, Ellard."

"Good. Have some bread."

"You know what we forgot?"

"No, what?"

"An enormous pot of really strong tea."

Amused, Ellard went into the kitchen, and Andria sat back with a sigh of near repletion, while her eyes wandered slowly round the room. They fell on a large bookcase, bulging with volumes of every shape and size, some of them with thick leather bindings. Had Ellard combed the antique shops for those, she wondered?

He came back carrying a fat steaming teapot in one hand and two mugs in the other. He put them down, grinning, then disappeared again, returning with milk and sugar.

"Goodness, where did you get that milk jug?" Andria asked. "It says 'A Present from Blackpool'."

"Well, it was, in a way," Ellard said. "I won it in a shooting gallery."

"Did you really? I never win anything like that. Would you like me to pour?"

"Yes please." He watched her, leaning back in his chair, then asked: "Now what happened, Andy? I know something did. You didn't have a wedding invitation from your mother, by any chance?"

100

"No, worse than that. Oliver was waiting for me when I got home last night, to ask me to go. I told him no and practically threw him out."

"I see." He was frowning and looking thoughtful. "Well, that's a natural reaction, I suppose, Oliver should have expected it. But Andy, have you really thought things through? It sounds heartless, but in a way it might be as well if you went, if only to clear them both out of your system."

She stared at him, milk jug in hand, and there was silence for a long moment. Then she swallowed hard, and asked:

"Have you been invited?"

"Yes, I have, and I'll have to go, Andy, if only because your mother is an old friend and Oliver is appearing in one of my productions."

"Yes, I can see that." Andria stared down at the table. "But it isn't just what I *ought* to do, Ellard — I just don't think I can do it."

She looked up at him, tears in her eyes, and he put his hand over hers, holding it tightly.

"If you're afraid of making a fool of yourself, everyone does at weddings," he said gently. "And I'll be there, giving you moral support. Think it over, will you? I honestly think it would be better if you did."

"You may be right," she acknowledged. "I — I'll think about it."

"Good. Now let's go and sit down with this awful tea and make ourselves more comfortable, shall we? That settee's the best thing for relaxing on."

"Did you have that re-upholstered as well?" she asked, collecting the milk jug and sugar basin and putting them down on the small table he indicated.

Ellard gave a graphic description of the settee before he rescued it, and Andria shuddered.

"And the spring stuck in just underneath your shoulder blades?" she asked. "Awful!"

"Excruciating," he agreed. "But it's all right now."

It was, and she lay back against it, smiling almost dreamily at him.

"You are nice, Ellard," she said, suddenly. "You and Suky — I don't know what I'd have done without you."

She had intended her kiss to be friendly, but as she leaned over to bestow it on his cheek, he turned his head and their lips met. His arms came round her in a tight, possessive grip, and he pulled her on to his knees. For a startled moment she resisted, then suddenly realisation came to her — Ellard's feelings for her had nothing to do with friendship or even affection, it was much, much more than that . . . she found herself kissing him back, her hands locked round his neck, until, breathless, they drew apart and stared at each other.

Ellard gave a lopsided smile.

"Sorry, Andy," he said, his voice hoarse. "I didn't mean that to happen — not yet, anyway . . ."

"I — it's all right," Andria found her own voice.

Her heart was thudding its way through her ribs, and as she slid slowly away from Ellard she realised that something momentous had happened — relations between them could never be the same again. In two short minutes Ellard had ceased to be merely a friend and become a potential lover . . . "

"Well," Ellard said, and there was a laugh in his voice. "That's the first time I've made a pass at a girl on top of a fish and chip supper — I've always understood the proper thing was champagne and caviare."

"I don't like caviar and champagne gets up my nose, Andria said, smiling. "And it was a very *nice* pass, Ellard."

"I'm glad you think so," Ellard said, laughter crinkling his eyes at the corners. "I'd have hated it if you'd felt revolted."

"Far from it," Andria said quietly, and the laughter went from Ellard's eyes.

He looked searchingly at her face, and she looked back at him equally gravely, blue eyes intent.

"Well," Ellard said slowly. "Having established that you do like me, perhaps we can go on from there? Slowly?"

She nodded, suddenly shy.

"I'd like to see some of your books," she said, and he nodded.

"Right," he said briskly, and they went over to the bookcase.

It soon became apparent that Ellard had very wide literary tastes, and they ranged from modern novels to first editions over a hundred years old, some of which Andria felt sure were collectors' items.

"It must be nice to have room for this

sort of thing," she said, reluctantly handing back an ancient poetry book. "Suky and I just about have room for the basics like tables and chairs and beds . . . "

"Andria, I've been thinking," Ellard said abruptly. "Your flat . . . When did you say Suky was getting married and leaving?"

"In June," Andria replied. "Why, Ellard?"

"I was thinking about your rent," Ellard looked faintly embarrassed. "Will you be able to manage it? I take it you won't take any more money from Constance?"

"Certainly not," she said firmly. "Don't worry, Ellard, if I find I can't cope I'll look for something else, it'll be OK."

She put her hand on his arm to reassure him, and he covered the hand with his own, holding it tightly.

"Any difficulties and you'll let me know," he said. "Promise?"

"I promise," she nodded and he released her reluctantly.

It was then that she saw the clock on the mantelpiece and realised that it was after eleven.

"Ellard, I must go," she exclaimed. "It's

been a lovely evening. Could you ring for a taxi, please?"

"I'll do better, I'll take you home myself. No, don't argue, I'll get your coat."

They went out to his car, Andria shivering a little in the damp night air, still feeling bemused about what had happened. Ellard opened the car doors and she got in, slowly fastening her seat belt.

Ellard said very little on the drive back to Andria's flat, but he walked to the front door with her and kissed her goodnight. She sensed that he was restraining himself, and felt oddly grateful — he was giving her time, and as she prepared for bed she wondered how many men would be prepared to do that.

Suky had been right, but then she very often was.

But the next morning when they had breakfast together Andria discovered that she didn't want to talk about herself and Ellard, not even to Suky. Instead, they discussed the furnishings of the flat Suky and Bill were buying, and Suky showed Andria some brochures she had collected the day before.

"I like that suite best," Andria said, poring over them. "It looks comfortable and that's important when you've been working hard."

"You've picked the one Bill and I prefer, how strange," Suky exclaimed. "Just shows all great minds do think alike, doesn't it?"

Andria giggled, then turned her attention to the china brochure.

"Some of these are lovely," she said, pointing to a dinner service. "By the way, Suky, what *do* you want for a wedding present?"

"Funny you should ask that," Suky's eyes twinkled mischievously. "Bill and I got out a list yesterday — here it is . . . "

"Worked very hard, didn't you?" Andria said, smiling. "Now then . . . put me down for the coffee set, will you? Which design and what colours?"

Suky stated a preference, and Andria made a note in her diary.

"Have you thought about your wedding dress yet?" she asked.

"I've seen one I liked," Suky said. "Will you come out shopping and help me choose?"

"I'd love to," Andria exclaimed, and then she remembered that she hadn't told Suky about Oliver's visit, and did so quickly.

Suky stared at her in open-mouthed disbelief.

"I can't *credit* that they'd actually think you'd go!" she exclaimed. "Haven't they *any* idea of the way you'd feel? Has anyone else been asked?"

"Ellard has, he told me so," Andria got up. "Suky, I'll have to go, or I'll be late. See you tomorrow morning. Perhaps we can fix up a shopping date then."

"Is Ellard going?" Suky asked, frowning, and Andria nodded.

"He'll have to, Oliver's one of his actors, and Constance is an old friend," she said. "He — he thinks it might be advisable if I went, too — I've got a feeling there are some rumours floating about he wouldn't mind being scotched."

"I expect there are," Suky said cynically. "He could be right, I suppose — but it would be an awful ordeal for you, Andy. Do you think you could do it?"

"I — I might," Andria said slowly. "I told Oliver no, of course, but I can see Ellard's point — I'm still thinking about it."

Suky said no more, but her shapely lips were tucked in tightly, as if she was biting back a blistering comment.

Andria thought it over for several more days, and neither Ellard or Suky mentioned the matter again. To her surprise, Ellard invited herself, Suky and Bill out in a foursome, and while they were having dinner he gave Suky and Bill a wedding present, a little antique jug.

"Oh, Ellard, that's lovely!" Suky exclaimed, holding it up to the light. "You — you shouldn't have. Isn't it beautiful, Bill? I didn't expect anything, Ellard — you — you don't really know us all that well."

"I know you very well," Ellard said, smiling. "I know you because of what Andria has told me." His gaze went to Bill. "I think you're a very lucky guy."

"I think so, too," Bill said, gripping Suky's hand. "Thanks, Ellard."

"You must come out with us," Suky said, stroking the jug gently before re-wrapping it. "We'll have to arrange a time."

"That's not easy, believe me," Bill said "What with Suky on night duty and me getting my flights changed and all that sort of thing."

"Life can be very hectic," Ellard agreed, and Andria remembered that he had been all the way to Edinburgh — and back — in a day on some business trip recently, then back to the theatre the next day without apparently even getting tired.

"If we can all fit into the flat I'll make dinner one evening, if you'll risk my cooking," she said, tentatively, wondering if Ellard would agree. "Suky can fix it with you, Bill, and I can fix it with Ellard."

"Great," Bill exclaimed, and Ellard nodded. "So brush up your menus, my dear!"

"Andria's cooking's OK." Suky defended her friend. "She just pretends she can't do anything but act, but she can, I promise you."

"Annie's the one," Andria said. "She should have been a professional chef."

"You'd think with all that good food inside him Nigel would be kindlier than he is sometimes," Ellard observed, reaching for the wine bottle, and Andria nodded agreement.

She had heard Nigel herself that morning, making an acid remark to his understudy, and Ellard had obviously heard him, too.

"Is there much of that sort of thing in the theatre? Bitchiness, I mean?" Bill asked, and Ellard shrugged.

"Not in my productions, if I can help it," he said. "Too distracting. But you have to allow for a certain amount of strain as well — it isn't easy."

"No, I don't suppose it is," Bill's brown eyes were thoughtful. "Beats me how Andria goes on being such a sweetie."

She knew then that Suky had told Bill about Oliver and Constance, but she didn't mind — Bill was no gossip and if Suky had asked him to hold his tongue then he would.

"I've got Suky to talk to, that's what helps," Andria smiled, and a sudden wave of unhappiness swept over her — she and Suky were as close as sisters, closer than some, and the flat would be horribly empty when she was married and gone . . .

"Andria's going to be my bridesmaid,"

Suky said, and Andria forced a smile, hoping that her expression had not revealed her thoughts. Constance had warned her once that she had a most expressive face . . .

"Ah," Ellard grinned. "I hope I'm invited to the whoop up afterwards."

"You're invited to the whole thing," Bill grinned back. "And don't invent some excuse, because it won't be accepted."

"I shouldn't dream of inventing an excuse," Ellard said. "Especially as Andria is bridesmaid — what colour is your dress, Andy!"

"That's a closely guarded secret," she said solemnly. "Isn't it, Suky?"

"Certainly it is," Suky said. "But she'll look so gorgeous I shall have to watch she doesn't look better than me!"

Watching Bill and Suky together, Andria's feeling of sadness went. They were so ideally suited, so deeply in love, that nothing else seemed relevant, and she smiled to herself. Then she caught Ellard's eye, and realised that he was looking at her, and that his guard was down . . . She knew then that Ellard loved her, and not just with passion, but with everything else which goes to make up a relationship. She drew a slightly ragged breath — sooner or later she was going to have to make up her mind about Ellard, and at that moment in time she didn't know how she felt. Attracted? More than that?

Ellard looked away, making some remark about the decor in the restaurant, and asking if Suky and Bill had come to any decision about their own colour schemes. Conversation became general, and Andria joined in, until Suky said reluctantly that they ought to leave. Ellard looked at his watch and nodded.

"It's been a great evening, Ellard," Bill said, beaming. "Thanks, Ellard."

"Bill, I believe you're a bit tipsy!" Suky exclaimed, and Bill grinned, slightly shame-faced.

"Maybe a little bit," he said, and then Andria remembered Suky mentioning once that Bill had absolutely no head for alcohol whatsoever.

He walked quite steadily to the car, however, and flopped into the back seat with Suky, while Andria silently took her place beside Ellard. Her mind had flashed to the little vase he had given Suky — how much had he paid for it, she wondered?

"I'll drop you girls off, then I'll deposit Bill," Ellard said as he started the car. "It's been a great evening."

"Super," Bill said loudly from the back of the car.

Andria heard Ellard suppress a chuckle, and smiled in sympathy. Bill might be a little tight, but at least he was nice with it . . .

Upstairs in the flat Suky took a long breath and fished out her vase again.

"Honestly, Andy," she said. "It was so sweet of him, and it must have cost a bomb . . . He is nice, isn't he? And he thinks worlds of you, and don't tell me he doesn't, I saw him looking . . . What will you say when he proposes?"

"*If* he proposes," Andria said, but Suky was not to be put off.

"I said *when,*" she insisted. "What will you do?"

"Oh, Suky, I — I don't know," Andria dropped into a chair and ran her hands through her thick hair. "I like him very much, he's been so kind, but after Oliver . . . "

114

"You just put that — that *snake* out of your mind," Suky said grimly. "Ellard's worth ten of him. Now, what shall I do to keep you safe, you pretty thing?"

Eventually she rolled the vase up in a silk scarf and placed it tenderly in a drawer, while Andria silently considered what she had said. Suky was right, of course she was, it would be infinitely more sensible to try and forget Oliver than go on thinking about him, but it was easier said than done, and what about the wedding invitation? Should she accept it? Was Ellard right? Uncannily, Suky seemed to follow her thoughts.

"I read somewhere that if you hated somebody you tied yourself to them in the worst possible way," she said suddenly. "It took me a long time to understand that but I think it's true, Andy. Maybe you should go to that wedding and then forget them both altogether. Think about it."

"I've thought," Andria said, looking up with a rueful smile. "You're right, Suky, and so is Ellard. It'll kill me to do it, but I will. I'll go to Con and Oliver's wedding."

6

ANDRIA told Ellard of her decision the next morning, having waited an opportunity to get him on his own. He looked at her for a moment as if he hadn't quite realised what she'd said, then his face broke into a smile.

"Good." He took her hand and squeezed it hard. "I'm sure it's the right thing, Andy."

"You — you will be there, won't you, Ellard?" she asked, and he bent quickly and kissed her cheek.

"All the time," he said reassuringly. "Don't worry about that. Will you write to Con and tell her, or shall I mention it when I see her next time? It might be better if you wrote, Andy."

Andria nodded, then moved away as someone called out to Ellard. Well, she'd done it now, she couldn't back out, though how she would get through the day she simply didn't know . . .

It was Suky who said that she should

think of it as a part she was playing, not as something that was actually happening, and Andria decided she might be right.

"And wear something especially attractive," Suky said, flinging open the door of the wardrobe they shared. "Can you afford a new outfit? Not really? Well, then . . . "

They turned out all Andrea's clothes, finally deciding on a mustard yellow linen suit with a matching blouse.

"Your shoes are fine," Suky said, a tan court shoe in one hand and a sandal in the other. "What about a hat? Not strictly necessary, of course, but it might be nice, especially if they're getting married in church."

"They're not, it's a registry office," Andria said. "And I haven't got a hat."

Suky dived into her half of the wardrobe, rummaged around, and came out clutching a hat box.

"Look in there," she ordered. "There might be something."

Andria looked, and discovered a little straw hat with streamer ribbons in exactly the right shade. She put it on, while Suky stood back and surveyed her critically, head on one side.

"That's *super,*" she said. "Just right, and it doesn't hide your face or your hair. Good. Have you written to your mother yet?"

"M'm. It wasn't much of a letter, I just said I was coming with Ellard. What do I do about a present, Suky?"

"Don't know." For once Suky looked blank. "I suppose they *will* expect one?"

"Well, it'll look awfully odd if I don't give them anything. After all, this is partly a cover-up."

"I see your point. Can I think about it for a bit?"

Andria nodded, hopeful that Suky might come up with a bright idea, and fairly quickly. The wedding was set for May 1st, and that was only three days from now. There was another consideration, too — Andria had sent her mother's cheque back, but it had left a large hole in her finances, and there wasn't a lot to pay for anything . . .

She looked through her own possessions, hoping that there was something she might part with, but could find nothing suitable, and finally she confided her dilemma to Ellard, who nodded understandingly.

"What do you give somebody who has

absolutely everything, including gold taps on the bath?" she asked, grinning wryly.

"I was wondering that myself," Ellard grinned back. "But I found a book, a first edition . . . want me to have a quick look round for you?"

"Oh, would you? I was wondering about silver — something antique, and you know much more about that than I do. Only — " a faint flush mounted in her cheeks — "I can't afford *too* much, Ellard . . . "

"Leave it with me. There's a shop I frequent and I'm well in with the manager. Yes, Charlie, we're coming . . . "

They went back to rehearsals, and Andria felt conscious of a weight off her mind. Ellard would find something.

"The next evening he drove her home, and as he parked the car he said suddenly:

"Andria, I almost forgot — I've managed to find a present, a George the Third six-bottle cruet, just ideal, I'm sure you'll like it."

Andria looked at him, and gulped.

"How — how much?" she faltered, her heart sinking.

"I managed to get it cheaply as the marks were a bit rubbed," Ellard said.

"It was three hundred and fifty pounds."

Andria gave a strangled gasp, and Ellard looked at her, apparently surprised.

"What's the matter, Andy?" he asked, and then she saw that he was laughing.

"Oh, Ellard, you — you *pig!*" she cried, weak with relief, and he stopped laughing and said:

"Well, I did see it, and it was gorgeous, but as I didn't want to put you in my debt for the rest of the year, I got this instead."

He reached into the back of the car and produced a padded parcel, which he handed to her.

"It's a bit later and a bit less money," his eyes were dancing wickedly. "Would a hundred and fifty pounds fit the bill better?"

"Much better. Don't ever play a trick like that on me again. Do you realise it'll take me about three months to pay you back?"

"Good, I like having you in my debt," Ellard leered hideously. "Only don't worry about it . . . Aren't you going to invite me in for coffee?"

"I might if you behave — I *might* even offer you supper."

"I'll eat anything," Ellard said hopefully, and Andria led him upstairs, clutching the parcel.

"What is it?" she asked, and Ellard said:

"It calls itself a silver cruet stand, and it's hallmarked 1906. Have a look at it and tell me if you like it."

She looked, while he watched her face to gauge her reactions.

"Ellard, it's lovely," she exclaimed. "Thank you for getting it — I just wish — " she stopped, biting her lips.

"You just wish what?" he asked.

"I wish I was giving it with love, not just because I — I've got to," she blurted, and Ellard put both arms round her in a hard, unexpected hug.

"Never mind, you're doing the right thing," he said.

"We've worn that expression out," Andria said, her voice muffled in his shoulder. "'The right thing'. I don't want to hear that for a long time, not after it's over."

"Well it soon will be," Ellard kissed the top of her head, then released her. "Andy, I'm starving — I really *will* eat anything!"

"Wait a minute, I'll check the fridge."

She went into the kitchen, and Ellard sat down slowly, his face thoughtful. After a moment she put her head round the door.

"Macaroni cheese?" she enquired, and he nodded.

"Can I come and watch you make it?" he asked, and she nodded.

He sat on the edge of the table, talking about the way the play was going, then, unexpectedly, he said:

"Andy, could you assume a convincing American accent if you had to?"

"I don't know, I've never tried," Andria stopped stirring the macaroni, interested. "Why?"

"I was thinking of doing a play in New York and taking you with me," he said slowly. "Not at once, of course, but perhaps later in the year when we know this one is safely launched. Would you come?"

"Yes, I would." Andria nodded. "But I'm not sure about the accent, Ellard — it would have to sound authentic and aren't there different ones?"

"There sure are," Ellard said, sounding like a Texas cowboy. "But you'd come and that's what I wanted to know . . . watch it,

Andy, that stuff's boiling over!"

Andria whisked her saucepan out of danger, and Ellard went on to describe the play. It sounded a distinct possibility, and she wondered not for the first time how Ellard thought of all the things he did and where he got all his energy from.

"It's not all my idea," he explained. "Remember my American friend? He came up with it a couple of weeks ago — sent me a script, as a matter of fact. It's pretty good. We don't need to do it right away, he's busy on something else, but as I said, later on this year. Can I grate that cheese for you?"

They ate hungrily together, their knees almost touching, and as they talked Andria almost forgot the ordeal before her.

"You're a very *interesting* person, Ellard," she said, as she made their coffee. "Not a bit like anyone else I know."

"Unique, that's me," Ellard said smugly. "You make a very good cup of coffee, Andy, just right . . . "

Before he left they discussed the arrangements for travelling to the wedding, and he said he would call for her at nine o'clock in the morning promptly.

ADH9

"We can't leave it any later if we're to get there in time," he said. "On the other hand, we don't want to get there too soon and have to make small talk, especially in the circumstances."

"In and out as quickly as ever we can?" Andria suggested, smiling faintly.

"I think so," Ellard nodded. "We can always plead pressure of work."

He gave her an encouraging hug and left, and as she got slowly ready for bed she wondered how many people would read the message on her present. "Best wishes from Andria". Not very warm, but she simply hadn't been able to write "love" or anything else. Perhaps Constance wouldn't expect it.

Suky had suggested she take something to make her sleep that night, and though Andria disliked sleeping pills she did take two as advised, and slept very soundly, so soundly that she barely heard the alarm go off, and it was Suky who roused her.

"Come on, love," she said, shaking Andria's shoulder. "It's half-past eight, you'll be late."

"Oh, good heavens!"

Andria scrambled out of bed and shot into the shower, shedding her nightie on the way. Suky picked it up with a sympathetic smile, and when her friend was dressed produced a cup of tea and a slice of toast which she insisted on Andria having.

"And *sit down,*" she commanded. "You've got ten minutes before Ellard arrives, and you look very nice. Super, in fact . . . "

"I wish you were coming, Suky," Andria said thickly through a mouthful of buttered toast.

"I'm glad I'm not," Suky said grimly. "I couldn't trust myself not to have a dig at the pair of them. No, the crust as well, you've got time."

Andria obeyed, and admitted later to Ellard that she was glad she had.

"Everyone feels better with something inside them," Suky said, as Andria disappeared to clean her teeth. "It's a well known medical fact."

Andria was arranging her hat over her auburn curls when they heard Ellard's car draw up outside. They exchanged glances, and Suky said "good luck", giving Andria a shove in the direction of the door.

"Go on, you look great," she said encouragingly. "Got the present? Good."

Andria fled, knowing that if she didn't go quickly then her nerve would fail her and she wouldn't be able to go at all.

Ellard was holding the car door open for her, and his eyes widened approvingly as she scrambled in beside him.

"You look terrific," he said. "Absolutely right . . . How do you feel?"

"Well, Suky fed me and I did sleep," Andria returned his smile. "All right, I guess . . . and you look pretty good yourself, Ellard. I love the carnation."

"There's one for you on the back seat," he said, starting the car. "We can put it on when we stop for coffee."

She sat beside him, and her mind went back unbidden to the last time she had driven on this particular route. Oliver had been beside her then, tense and eager, burning to get on with his career, and like a fool she had wanted to help him . . . sudden tears stung her eyes, and she blinked them angrily away. Self-pity wouldn't help — what was needed now was self-discipline. There would be eyes on her as well as Constance, and the only way she could carry the situation off was by keeping cool and behaving as though nothing untoward was happening.

"We'll go straight to the Registry Office," Ellard said, swinging the car expertly round a tight corner. "That will avoid the crowd at Con's house, if there is a crowd, that is. I've a feeling they might have kept their guest list to a minimum."

"You may be right," Andria agreed. "Well, we'll soon find out."

Ellard insisted on stopping halfway along the road for a coffee, and to Andria's reluctant amusement he pressed biscuits on her as well.

"Remember what Napoleon said about an army marching on its stomach," he grinned. "Eat them and don't argue."

"I'm surrounded by bossy people," Andria complained, but she picked up a biscuit and nibbled it, wishing fervently that the whole thing was over.

She wished it still more when they parked the car as near to the Registry Office as they could get. There was a crowd gathered outside the swing doors, brightly dressed guests, reporters with notepads and cameras, and a knot of people who were obviously sight-seers, all staring curiously at the couple posing before them.

Ellard looked at Andria and grimaced.

"Well, this is it," he muttered, pressing her hand encouragingly. "Come on, darling. Stick close to me and we'll be OK."

Hand in hand they walked towards the office, and for a panic-stricken moment Andria wanted to turn and run. Then she caught sight of her mother, and sheer admiration kept her from doing that. Constance looked beautiful. Tall and slender in a long shimmering dress which appeared to be made of cloth of gold, holding a sheath of golden lilies, she stood smiling beside Oliver, who looked highly nervous but very well dressed in a grey smartly cut suit. He was sporting a white carnation on his lapel and smiling resolutely, but he looked anything but comfortable, and the baser part of Andria gave a silent snarl of satisfaction. Let him wriggle, he deserved it!

"I give her full marks," Ellard remarked dispassionately, his lips close to Andria's ear. "Talk about colours to the mast!"

To her own astonishment Andria felt herself grin, and then Constance caught sight of her and the smile froze on her lips for one tell-tale moment. Then it came back and she called:

"Andy, *darling!* And Ellard! We were beginning to think you couldn't make it."

"I wouldn't have missed this for anything," Ellard replied, a sort of gentle malice in his tone. "You look superb, Con — hello, Oliver, how are you?"

"Hollow," Oliver said, with a sickly smile. "Hello Andy. How are you?"

"Fine," Andria said, gazing defiantly into his eyes. "Just fine. Oh, yes, of course . . . "

She turned, smiling automatically as one of the reporters aimed his camera at her, and Ellard said, glancing quickly at his watch:

"Shouldn't we be going in, Con?"

"You're right, we should." Constance turned to Oliver with a quick smile. "Darling, are you ready?"

"Of course." Oliver took her hand and slid it into his arm. "Come on then, everyone."

Ellard had been right, Andria thought as she fell into step behind her mother —

they *had* kept the guest list down. Apart from herself and Ellard, there were only about ten other guests. Michael Lester was there with Polly, there were one or two other actors, Constance's agent, and some other people Andria didn't know. Perhaps Constance *was* embarrassed — was it the difference in her age and Oliver's? Andria had to admit that it wasn't at all noticeable, in fact Constance looked radiant and nowhere near her actual age, while Oliver looked tense and strained. Did he expect Andria to make some sort of scene? If so, let him think it for a bit longer . . .

"You're doing fine," Ellard whispered to her as they took their places. "Keep it up, this doesn't take long."

He was right, it didn't, and by resolutely making her mind a blank Andria kept smiling, though she felt as they made their way back into the sunshine that her face had set in an imbecilic, meaningless grin.

But she brushed her mother's soft cheek with her lips, posed again for the photographers, and went back to the car with Ellard, who had discovered that the reception was being held at Constance's house. A little train of cars moved away from the Registry Office, and Andria sat back in her seat, momentarily closing her eyes.

"Great," Ellard said quietly. "Well done. Nobody could have told there was anything wrong."

"Michael and Polly knew," Andria said flatly. "They must have done."

"They won't talk," Ellard said, with quiet conviction. "There won't be awkward questions from the reporters after this. It's a buffet lunch so we can mingle a bit, then leave."

"M'm," Andria nodded.

She felt exhausted already, and Ellard shot her a quick, concerned look.

"What you need is a drink," he said. "Let's hope Con's laid on plenty of booze."

She had, and plenty of food as well. Andria found herself, plate and fork in hand, talking earnestly to a middle-aged man who turned out to be a theatre critic mainly known for his waspish reviews. To her surprise Andria found him charming, kindly even, and she talked to him for nearly a quarter of an hour, until Polly came over and interrupted them with her wide, friendly smile.

"Have you been round the garden, Andy?" she asked, as the critic moved off to join another chattering group. "It's lovely, shall we have a wander?"

Andria swallowed the last of her chicken vol au vent and nodded. Her head was beginning to ache, and she stepped into the fresh air with a little sigh of relief.

Polly waited until they were out of earshot, then turned to Andria, her eyes full of sympathetic concern "Are you all right, love?" she asked. "Michael and I didn't think you'd come."

"I almost didn't, but Ellard and Suky persuaded me to. There's been gossip and he was afraid the newspapers would get hold of the story."

"Yes, they tried to question Michael a few days ago but he gave them a brush-off," Polly said, her lips tightening. "I think you did the right thing, Andy. The rumours will die down now, I'm sure."

Andria nodded, feeling that if she heard the words "the right thing" just once more she would either scream or hit someone.

"Shall we really look at the garden?" she asked, and Polly nodded agreement.

They were admiring a flowering shrub

when Ellard abruptly appeared, looking at his watch.

"Sorry, Andy darling, but I have to get back," he said apologetically. "I know it's a bore but could you possibly come now?"

"Yes, of course, Andria picked up her cue smoothly. "It's been lovely seeing you again, Polly."

"And you," Polly said, hugging her. "Take care of yourself and the best of luck with the play."

They stepped back into the big lounge, Ellard's hand on her arm, and Constance turned to exclaim, her voice beautifully balanced between affection and regret:

"Darling, must you go? No, it's all right, we do understand, don't we, Oliver? Now listen, please take some champagne, there's masses of it here, far too much for us. No, Ellard, I insist . . . Andy, darling, your present was lovely, wasn't it, Oliver? And you look quite lovely. No, Oliver, give him another bottle — that's right . . . You can drink it at home, not in the car."

"Don't worry, we won't get tight while I'm driving," Ellard said, smiling. "Goodbye, everyone — have a great party."

All the guests trooped outside to see

them leave, and as she turned in her seat for a last glimpse of her mother and Oliver she saw that their hands were tightly clasped, as if for mutual support.

Ellard said nothing for a few minutes, then he gave a long ragged sigh.

"Phew, thank God that's over," he said. "I shouldn't like to go through that again . . . Did you see that one reporter, Andy? He had a face like an intelligent weasel — I was dreading being questioned by him, he looked as if he'd know exactly what to ask."

"I'm just glad it's finished," Andria said, tiredly. "It's all rather a blur now . . . "

"Yes," Ellard nodded, then, suddenly, he gave a mischievous little boy grin. "Let's go home to my place and get roaring drunk."

"That's not a bad idea," Andrea grinned back. "Well, maybe not *roaring* drunk, just *mellow*."

"Mellow will do just fine," Ellard said. "And we'll have dinner, too."

They stopped at a Chinese take-away and collected some food, and as Andria stepped into Ellard's flat she sighed with relief.

"It's so *nice* here, Ellard," she said, as she dumped the succulent smelling packages on the kitchen table, while Ellard carefully deposited the champagne in the fridge to cool. "I really like your flat."

"Good, because I like you in it," Ellard said, drawing her into his arms, where she relaxed with another sigh. "You were terrific today, Andy, I felt proud of you.

"I couldn't have managed without you," she lifted her face for his kiss. "We did carry it off well, didn't we?"

"M'm." Ellard released her reluctantly. "Andy, I'm starving — shall we eat?"

They sat opposite each other, enjoying a leisurely meal, sipping champagne and talking. Andria relaxed completely, thankful that the painful hurdle had been taken and the whole thing was *over* . . .

"I must say Con chose some terrific champagne," Ellard remarked, bottle in hand. "Want another glass?"

"Why not?" Andria smiled dreamily at him. "Supposed to be a celebration, isn't it?"

"Mm-hum." Ellard tipped the bottle and poured, and bubbles rose to the surface and popped. "Sure is."

"Have some more bean sprouts," Andria suggested, and Ellard looked sharply at her.

"Andy, are you tight?" he asked.

She considered the question gravely for a moment, then shook her head.

"Not yet," she said, and giggled. "Bottoms up."

"But of course."

Ellard tossed his drink off and poured himself another.

"A toast," he said. "To the bride and groom."

"Right. The bride and groom."

"I think I'll get the other bottle," Ellard said, and rose carefully from his chair. "We might as well finish it all up, mightn't we?"

"Very wasteful not to," Andria agreed. "Might go flat in the fridge, mightn't it?"

"Might get lonely," Ellard said, returning with the bottle. "Here we go then. . . . "

Andria surveyed her glass squiffily. Somewhere in the dim recesses of her mind she realised that she was drinking too much, but somehow it didn't seem important.

"Let's drink to the play," she said. "Let's

136

drink to a big success."

"The play," Ellard rose to his feet, and Andria lurched clumsily to hers. "May it be a tremendous theatrical achievement . . . "

"And huge returns at the booking-office," Andria flopped back into her chair. "Oops!"

"One more glass each and it's gone," Ellard held up the bottle. "You game, Andy?"

"Sure," she nodded. "Why not?"

Ellard refilled their glasses with exaggerated care, then raised his.

"To us," he said, and Andria nodded.

"To us," she said, and they linked arms and drank . . .

7

ANDRIA rolled drowsily over in bed, half opened her eyes, then closed them again, savouring the feeling of the soft sheets against her naked body. What was the time? She would have to get up in a minute, but meanwhile this bed was very comfortable . . .

Too comfortable . . .

Her eyes snapped wide open, she looked round the room, suddenly wide awake. There was something strange about it, something unfamiliar, and it seemed to have grown larger during the night . . . and then with a shock, realisation dawned — it wasn't the small cramped room she shared with Suky, it was the bedroom in Ellard's flat, and it was Ellard's big comfortable bed she was in. Her heart began to pound as her hand moved instinctively to the right, exploring . . .

It encountered a long shape lying beside her, and as she turned her head the shape heaved itself over and became Ellard, apparently as naked as herself, his hair hanging over one eye and a faint growth of bristle sprouting on his chin.

"Hi," he said softly, and a grin appeared on his face, half triumphant and half deprecating. "Did you sleep well?"

She stared at him speechlessly, struggling wildly with a memory which seemed very reluctant to return. What had happened? Her brain seemed stuffed with soggy cotton wool, but after a moment she seemed to recall being carried into the bedroom and dumped on the bed . . .

"We — we had too much to drink," she said, and Ellard nodded, then winced a little.

"Yes, we did," he agreed. "Much too much."

She was clutching the sheet to her, still staring at him, and suddenly a question tore through her mind — had anything else happened? Judging by Ellard's expression it had . . .

She bit her lip, colour flooding into her face, and Ellard sat up suddenly and put his arms round her. It was an almost protective gesture and she hid her hot face in his shoulder, feeling it warm and strong to her touch.

"You can't remember, can you?" he asked gently. "It doesn't matter, Andy — what does matter is that I love you. Will you marry me?"

She should have expected that, but it still came as a suprise, and she kept silent for a moment, her thoughts churning and racing to and fro in her mind. Ellard loved her, she knew that, and he was a sincere and honest man, whom she liked very much indeed, so why not? Why not make him happy and try to snatch some happiness for herself?

She had been deeply in love with Oliver, and where had it got her? Betrayal, heartache and misery . . . She would be safe with Ellard, and she knew without doubt he was the faithful type. When Ellard loved, he would stay loving . . .

She lifted her face and looked into his.

"Yes, Ellard, I will," she said quietly, and watched his eyes light up.

Then his lips met hers, gently at first, then more urgently and as her arms slid round his neck she knew the decision was taken, and there was no going back.

They were late at the theatre that morning, but as they walked hand in hand on to the stage a battery of knowing eyes turned on them, and Andria blushed, glancing nervously at Ellard, who gazed blandly at his assembled cast, coughed, then said:

"An announcement, folks — Andy and I are engaged."

There was a chorus of "There, I told you so!" "Congratulations!" "When's the wedding?" and Andria found herself being hugged and kissed and in the case of Yvonne and her understudy, cried over.

"I *knew* it would happen," Yvonne sobbed happily. "Isn't it *wonderful?*"

"Great," Nigel sounded totally sincere for once, and Charlie, who had been pounding Ellard painfully on the back, stopped and beamed round at everyone.

"We must have a drink," he pronounced. "Has anyone got anything?"

Someone produced a bottle of lemonade and someone else a brandy flask, and they toasted Andria and Ellard in this strange mixture, while everyone talked at once and nobody listened to anything anyone else said.

It was Ellard who finally called them to

order and rehearsals began. Andria realised with a shock that their opening night was less than a week away, and wondered how she was going to fit everything in. There was Suky's wedding too, they must go to that, and Ellard had made it clear that the sooner their own marriage took place the happier he would be.

"It needn't be a big affair, need it?" Andria had asked in the car on the way to the theatre. "I mean, I can hardly ask Con to organise it, not in the circumstances. I know it sounds odd, Ellard, most girls seem to want a white wedding with all the trimmings, but would you be terribly disappointed if we chose a registry office?"

"Not at all, if that's what you would prefer," Ellard had replied, his hand covering hers for a moment. "We'll talk about it later, but it's OK by me, just as long as we *are* married. I've got this strange preference for legitimate children."

"That's odd, so have I," Andria smiled.

So he wanted children — She should have known he would, and somehow he rose in her estimation . . . Oliver hadn't, he'd told her so more than once . . .

She pushed Oliver resolutely out of her

mind. That was the past, it was the future that mattered . . .

"Speaking of Con, will you tell her or shall I?" Ellard asked. "I'll probably have to go north again soon, anyway."

"You tell her," Andria said, and he nodded.

How would Constance react to the news, Andria wondered? Would it come as a surprise? Somehow, she didn't think it would, but anyway, what did it matter? In future relations between her mother and herself would be cool but polite, and there was no need for them to meet except on formal occasions . . .

"Oh, Andy, that's *marvellous!*" Suky cried, her eyes shining. "I *knew* it, I always said so! I'm so pleased, you're just right for each other! Where are you going to live, in Ellard's flat, or will you buy a house?"

"In the flat for the time being, I think," Andria said. "Ellard's talking about going to New York soon, so maybe a house isn't a good idea at the moment."

"Well, it's a gorgeous flat, better than this poky hole," Suky said, looking disparagingly round their home. "And I *was* worried about you, Andy, here by yourself, and now you won't be, you'll have Ellard."

She was so obviously delighted that Andria's own spirits suddenly rose — it was all working out very well, even in her still over sensitive state she could see that, and she smiled back into Suky's radiant face.

"Will you come and help me choose my dress?" she asked, and Suky grinned.

"I was hoping you'd ask me that," she said. "I think a blue lace or maybe cream or turquoise would be lovely . . . "

A week later the play opened to good audiences, and judging by the reviews the next day it was very well received. As Charlie remarked complacently:

"Not bad at all, my dears, it should run for a year at least, don't you think so, Ellard?"

"Longer, I hope," Ellard's smile was full of quiet satisfaction. "Well done everyone . . . "

Andria was suffering from a sensation of anticlimax, so often experienced after a tense first night, but she smiled with the rest, and even Nigel refrained from any caustic remark. He looked tired, and

144

she wondered if he too, had been keyed up and anxious, but it turned out afterwards that Annie wasn't well and he was worried about her.

"What is it?" Andria asked when he told her later, and Nigel shrugged.

"Some sort of virus, the doctor thinks. She's resting at home now. She was pretty sick to miss the opening night."

"That is disappointing," Yvonne commiserated. "Still, she can come later, can't she? I'm sure we'll still be here."

"Hope so," Nigel smiled briefly, and rose rather stiffly from his stool. "Well, I'm off home, see you all this evening."

Andria and Ellard went out to lunch together, and it was over this meal that Ellard firmly pinned down the date of their wedding.

"Early in July," he said, and she experienced a sensation of near panic, which she quickly suppressed, nodding agreement.

"Fine," she said, and he reached across the table, gripping her hand hard.

"I can't wait," he said, smiling. "I'd say sooner but I know you want to get Suky's wedding out of the way first, and I ought to go over to the States and see Anthony Segall about that script we were talking about the other day.

"Did you want me to come too?" she asked, and he thought for a moment, then regretfully shook his head.

"I'd love it, but you got such a good review I think it would be wise for you to stay in the play for a few weeks longer," he said reluctantly. "I won't be gone for long, just a few days."

"I'll miss you," she said truthfully, and the grip on her hand tightened.

"I'll miss you, too," he said huskily. "You will take care of yourself while I'm gone? And promise me you won't walk home alone from the theatre late at night — get a lift or take a taxi."

"Promise," she nodded, and he released her hand reluctantly and sat back in his chair.

"Let's have coffee," he suggested. "And how about supper after the show tonight?"

She nodded, experiencing a sense of wonder at the way her life had altered over the past few weeks. Although she didn't know it, it was to change again dramatically quite soon . . .

It was Suky who pointed to the small column in the morning paper, frowning.

They were having a quick meal together, breakfast for Andria, supper for Suky, and as Suky passed the paper to her and Andria ran her eyes over it, a cold hand seemed to clutch at her stomach.

"New York theatre badly damaged by fire. Well known playwright injured."

"Isn't that the name of that friend of Ellard's?" Suky asked. "Anthony Segall! The one who's the part owner of the New York theatre."

"Yes, it is," Andria got slowly to her feet, her knees trembling a little. "Suky, I must phone and tell Ellard — it would be awful if he saw this before . . ."

As if on cue, the phone rang sharply, and with a quick glance at Suky, Andria went to answer it. Suky followed, hovering in the doorway, and guessing from the conversation that it was Ellard on the other end of the line.

"Yes, Ellard, I've seen it — how bad are things?"

There was a long pause, while Andria gnawed her bottom lip, then she said:

"I'm terribly sorry, darling, but at least

Anthony doesn't seem too bad, and you are insured. Yes, of course you must leave straight away — yes, I'll get myself to the theatre. You've told Charlie he's in charge? Good. Oh . . . yes, I understand. You have been busy, haven't you? No, it's all right. Yes, see you soon. Be careful . . . goodbye, darling."

She hung up slowly, then turned to Suky, pulling a rueful face.

"Anthony discovered the fire and tried to put it out by himself," she said, and Suky flung up her hands in horror. "He was in the theatre by himself and smelled burning. They think it might have been a cigarette but they're not quite sure."

"Faulty electrical wiring?" Suky suggested.

"Well, it could be," Andria said. "Fortunately when Anthony saw the thing was out of control he had the sense to call the fire brigade and get outside quickly, but he'd breathed in a lot of smoke and his hands were burned but not too badly. Ellard has gone to the airport as I expect you guessed. Suky, I must get ready for the theatre right away. Charlie will want a meeting at once, if I know him."

Suky nodded, and Andria hurried into

the bedroom, flinging off her dressing-gown and wondering exactly what Ellard would find when he arrived in New York.

"Thank goodness for insurance," she muttered as she turned on the shower, and then a disturbing thought occurred to her — insurance or not, any theatre loses money if nothing is playing in it — how long would the repairs take and how much would Ellard and Anthony lose while they were going on?

"Let us look on the bright side," Charlie said to his assembled and attentive audience. "Anthony will be all right, and the theatre was empty at the time. We must carry on here as though nothing has happened. Questions, anyone? No? Then let us adjourn for coffee."

He descended majestically from the small box he had been standing on, and Andria bit back a smile. There were times when Charlie only just escaped being pompous, and this was one of the times.

"He's right, of course, it could have been worse, Nigel said unexpectedly. "I was in a theatre where there was a fire once, and the auditorium was packed — not funny, I assure you."

"It wouldn't be," Charlie agreed. "Shall we go out for a bit, then, I could do with some fresh air."

Outside Andria stood breathing deeply. It was a lovely morning, fresh and sunny, the air unexpectedly soft after a heavy shower the night before. Nigel joined her on the pavement, and suddenly she remembered to ask him about Annie.

"Much better, thanks," he smiled briefly. "Come on, Andy, I'm dying for a coffee, and you must be, too. How did Ellard really take the news?"

"I think he was more concerned for his friend than anything else," she said, as they fell into step. "I must admit I thought about the money they would lose."

"That is a thought," Nigel said, turning down the corners of his mobile mouth. "Still, the show must go on, eh, Yvonne?"

"I'd like a pound for the number of times I've heard that," Charlie remarked, grinning. "Must be the oldest cliché in the business."

"One of them," Nigel admitted, grinning back, and suddenly Andria's spirits lightened — one thing was certain, no one in Ellard's London production was going to let him down, least of all herself . . .

It was late when she let herself into the flat that night, and as she climbed the stairs she stifled a yawn. The performance had gone very well, the audience had been appreciative, and Charlie had insisted on taking everyone out to supper afterwards, to make sure they all ate properly.

"Just like a nannie, my dear," Nigel said, *sotto voce*, and Andria had to admit he was right, Charlie did look like a male version of a nurse maid as he shepherded everyone towards the nearest restaurant.

"He means well," she whispered back, and Nigel gave his half mocking, half amused grin.

"I'd rather eat Annie's cooking," he said. "But anything to please the old boy."

"I think he's sweet," Yvonne said quietly, and Nigel grinned again, this time without the mockery.

Andria sat down on the bed, slowly taking off her shoes, wondering sleepily what Ellard was doing. Was it earlier or later in America? She could never remember . . . of course, it was earlier, so Ellard was probably still bustling around, trying to get everything sorted out.

He had given Charlie an address and a phone number, which must be the number of Anthony's flat — there wouldn't be any point in trying to get the theatre on the phone, it would be disconnected . . . She yawned again, and reached for the cold cream . . .

A week went by, and Andria had two scribbled communications from Ellard, obviously written in haste but full of affection. She wrote back, telling him everything as it happened, trying to be reassuring, not that there was any real need. Charlie was firmly in command and thoroughly enjoying it, and Helen backed him up, though occasionally her beautiful mouth twitched into a half hidden smile as if she was struggling hard not to laugh.

Suky managed to get a Saturday off work, and she and Andria shopped for Andria's wedding dress. It took three shops and two hours to make all the purchases, but eventually Andria decided on pale blue lace with matching accessories, and Suky agreed she had made the right choice.

"You're going to look beautiful," she said sincerely. "Absolutely super . . . Come on, let's go and have something to eat, or you'll be late for your matinee performance, and we can't have that, can we? Charlie will be having kittens."

"I'm sure they would be very aristocratic ones," Andria grinned. "The kind with the pedigree that sit and stare you out — you know."

They giggled all the way to the nearest cheap restaurant, and once again Andria realised how much she was going to miss Suky.

They parted outside the theatre, Suky carrying Andria's wedding clothes.

"No. I'll take them home for you." she said firmly. "Something might happen to them if you take them into the theatre with you. No, they're not too heavy, don't be daft . . . See you later."

Andria hurried inside, to be met by Nigel, who caught her arm.

"Can you get to the phone in Helen's room quickly, Andy," he said, and he was frowning. "It's Oliver . . . I'd have choked him off if I could but he says it's urgent. Something about Con — about your mother, Andy."

She stared at him open-mouthed for a moment, then almost ran in the direction of Helen's dressing-room, her heart beginning to thump painfully inside her. What did Oliver want? Why was he ringing her now? Was yet another disaster beginning to rear its ugly head? And why ring the theatre? What was wrong with the phone at her flat, surely that would have been more private?

With a feeling of impending doom, she reached Helen's door and tapped apprehensively on it.

"Come in," Helen called, and Andria entered, her eyes going straight to Helen's face.

"Here you are, my dear," Helen handed her the receiver, gave her an encouraging pat on the shoulder, and quietly left the room, closing the door soundlessly behind her.

"Hello," Andria said, and her voice must have sounded strange, because on the other end Oliver said:

"Is that you, Andy? Sorry about this,

154

but we've got a bit of a crisis this end —
Con — Con's not well, and her understudy
walked out last night . . . We were
wondering — could you possibly take over
the part?"

8

FOR a moment Andria thought her ears must be playing her tricks — take over a part from *Constance?*

"*What?*" she stammered finally, and Oliver repeated himself, his voice betraying tension and worry.

"But Oliver, how can I?" Andria took a deep breath. "For one thing, Ellard particularly wanted me to carry on here, and for another — well, I don't suppose for a moment I'd be equal to it, and I haven't learned the lines or anything . . . "

"I've had a word with Ellard already," Oliver said, and Andria's spine stiffened indignantly. "He's agreeable under the circumstances for you to step in, and your understudy's quite competent, isn't she? Please, Andy, think it over — it is important. Con's doctor says she can't carry on, and now the wretched understudy has left we can't think of anyone else who'll do for the part. It isn't easy but it could make your reputation as an actress, and

I'm not just saying that to influence you, it could."

"I see." Andria cradled the phone in her still slightly trembling hand, thinking, her teeth worrying her bottom lip.

Then something else occurred to her, and she said:

"Oliver, what about the — the age difference? Will it matter?"

"No, I don't think so," Oliver said, and it sounded as though he was holding himself very firmly in hand. "We've discussed it and we think it could be played by a woman of any age, provided she was a good actress — please, Andy, you'd be doing Ellard a favour, you know. He's already lost money in New York over this fire, if this play goes down the drain as well it could be a disaster."

"I — I'll have to speak to Charlie and Helen," Andria said, wavering.

"Yes, of course, I understand that," Oliver said. "But can you come up to Manchester quickly, Andria, tonight if possible. One of the girls is filling in for Con but she isn't really up to it. It's not fair on her and it's not fair to the rest of the cast, or the public either, and if this goes on much longer we'll start getting bad reviews and you know what that means."

"Only too well." Andria stood frowning, and then something else occurred to her — she had forgotten in her stunned suprise to ask what was the matter with Constance.

She did so, and there was an odd little pause. Then Oliver said guardedly:

"I — I'd rather not discuss it on the phone, Andy, but will you come and see us as soon as you get here? I'll give you our address and you can get a taxi from the station — and don't worry about the fares, I'll pay if you're short of money. Look, I'll have to go now — I'm due on stage in a few minutes, but please, Andy, we wouldn't be asking if it wasn't so important. Got a pencil? Then here's the address."

She scribbled obediently, still suffering a sense of unreality, and after another plea Oliver hung up, leaving Andria with the phone still clutched in her hand, her thoughts chaotic . . .

"Charlie," she thought. "I must speak to Charlie."

She found him in his dressing-room, quietly making up, and he took one look at her face, spun round on his stool, and listened quietly while she stumbled into speech.

"What shall I do, Charlie?" she asked, and he drew a deep breath.

"I think, my dear, that you will have to go," he said slowly. "And you had better go straight home and pack. Your understudy is here, I take it? Yes, of course she is, I saw her myself a few minutes ago. She's a good child, she'll cope . . . Give my love to your mother when you see her."

"Will you say goodbye to the others for me, Charlie?"

"Yes, of course I will, my dear." Charlie rose from his stool and kissed her. "Now go and the best of luck."

"Thanks, Charlie," she forced a smile. "I think I'm going to need it."

She hurried out of the theatre, and stood on the pavement for a moment, looking at the queue already forming outside the box office, fighting down sudden panic. What was she doing, rushing off to take over a part, following one of the best dramatic actresses in the country at a few days notice? And why had Con's understudy chosen this particular moment to desert? Had she been offered a part by someone else? That could be the explanation, because Con was usually very nice to her understudies in a casual sort of way . . . And what was the matter with Con, anyway? She usually enjoyed amazingly good health. Andria couldn't remember the last time her mother had been even mildly indisposed, so what had happened that was so serious her doctor had forbidden her to carry on with her part?

It must be something serious, Andria thought as she looked round for a taxi, and her inside did a little unexpected flip . . . she had thought she didn't care a damn about Constance, and it was a strange little shock to discover that after all, she did . . .

A cruising taxi drew up beside her and stopped, and Andria climbed in, settling herself against the cushions and willing herself to be calm. The next few days could be extremely hectic, and panicking wouldn't help at all.

The driver stopped and she paid him, forcing a smile, hurried to the door, opened it and climbed the stairs, wondering if

Suky was at home or not. She wasn't, but there was a note propped conspicuously against the clock, telling her that Suky had gone out with Bill.

Andria turned the paper over and scribbled a note in her turn, explaining briefly what had happened and promising to ring Suky as soon as she discovered what was going on. Then she went into the bedroom and packed, glancing briefly at her wedding dress hanging in the wardrobe, shrouded in a dress cover. It seemed ages ago that she and Suky had shopped for it, and yet it had only been that morning . . .

She zipped up her suitcase, took a last quick look round the room, then went down the stairs, carrying the case, thinking that it might have been more sensible to ring for a taxi than trust to the buses. Fortunately as she came out of the mews she saw one, empty and in search of a fare, and a few minutes later she was standing on the railway platform, waiting for the next train to Manchester, her thoughts still chaotic but outwardly composed.

Andria had always thought of Manchester as a grimy industrial city, not a very desirable place to live, but there was nothing shabby or down-at-heel about the top floor flat where Constance and Oliver were staying. It was situated in a pleasant tree-lined road, had large windows, was well decorated outside and appeared to overlook a park.

Andria looked at the little panel of bells outside the door, put her finger over the appropriate one and pressed, and a few minutes later the door opened and she recognised Edith Maggs, Con's one-time dresser and general domestic help.

"Hello, Edith," Andria said, smiling, and Edith looked her up and down as if she had not seen her for ten years at least.

"You've come then," she said ungraciously. "Go on up, and please be quiet — Miss Con's not at all *well.*"

"All right," Andria said meekly, and almost crept up the thickly carpeted stairs, Edith behind her. She would have liked to ask what Edith was doing there — she usually stayed in whatever house Constance was occupying at the time — obviously Con had felt justified in sending for her on this occasion, and Andria's stomach did another little twisting flip — something really *was* wrong to make her relinquish her caretaker's job and join Constance on location, as it were . . .

"She's in there," Edith indicated a door, giving Andria a fierce glare. "Don't you go upsetting her now, there's a good girl."

"I won't," Andria promised, thinking that there was a lot to be said for loyalty, and Edith was certainly loyal if nothing else.

Constance was propped up in bed, her magnificent hair streaming over the pillow in chestnut swathes, her face pale and her eyes heavy.

"Miss Andria, m'm," Edith murmured, giving Andria a final warning glance and retiring backwards, as if before royalty.

"Hello, Andy," Constance said, smiling wanly. "You came, then — thank you, darling."

Andria kissed her mother's soft cheek, stepped back and looked critically at her. To her surprise Constance didn't seem able to meet her eyes, and one hand was picking nervously at the sheet.

"I — I'm sorry about all this, Andy,"

Constance said. "Was Charlie very mad?"

"No, he sends his love," Andria said, a sense of puzzlement creeping over her.

Her mother quite obviously didn't have a cold or flu, or any sort of rash, so what was the matter with her?

"I've got the script here," Constance said, picking up a thick sheaf of papers and holding them out to Andria. "It's a difficult part, darling, but I think you can do it . . . yes, of course you can . . . Shall task Edith to get you some tea while you look at it?"

"Yes, please." Andria took the script, still feeling puzzled, and Constance picked up a little hand bell and tinkled it, reminding Andria of a female Oriental potentate summoning a minion to do her bidding.

Edith made no objection to making some tea for Andria, but when the tray came there was only one cup on it, and Andria looked enquiringly at her mother.

"Don't you want any, Con?" she asked and Constance pulled a face, half closing her eyes.

"I — I've gone *off* tea," she said, and Andria stared at her, milk jug in hand.

"But — but you love tea," she blurted.

"You used to drink quarts of it, and eat those really buttery scones, remember?"

This time Constance closed her eyes tightly, swallowing hard.

"Andria," she said imploringly. "If you have the least vestige of affection for me, don't mention buttery scones, *please!*"

Andria put her cup down carefully, took a deep breath, and asked:

"Constance, what *is* the matter with you?"

A wan smile crossed her mother's face.

"I thought you'd have guessed by now," she said ruefully. "I'm pregnant, I'm going to have a baby."

Andria stared at her, open-mouthed, too surprised to speak. Constance stared back at her, a half defiant, half pleading look on her face.

"Go on, laugh if you want to," she blurted. "Practically everyone else did."

"I — I haven't the least desire to laugh," Andria said. "I — I just wonder — I mean, Con, you're not stupid — how did you get caught like that? Were you careless or what?"

"Careless, stupid, whatever you like to call it," Constance's mouth curved into a reluctant smile. "I suppose everything happened so quickly I didn't *think* of anything like that . . . "

"I suppose it is that? I mean, are you sure?" Andria asked, and Constance nodded.

"Yes, it's been confirmed, I've had a test," she said. "But I think I knew already."

"But — but — " Andria's hand went to her forehead. "But what does Oliver think — feel about it?"

Oliver, who always insisted he didn't want children . . .

A sweet smile crossed her mother's face, transforming it into a vision of loving tenderness.

"He wants it every bit as much as I do," she said softly. "Which is why, Andy darling, that I have to do *everything* the doctor says or I may lose it, and this might be my very last chance to give Oliver a child. So here I am, stuck in bed, and that's why I sent for you. You're the only person we could think of who can cope with this part — even Ellard agrees with that."

Andria was silent, then another thought struck her.

"Why did your understudy leave?" she asked.

"I think it was my fault," Constance looked guilty. "I was feeling so ill I'm afraid I was really *bitchy* to her, and then someone offered her a small part in a film, and off she went. Very inconvenient but I couldn't really blame her. I hope she makes a success of her part, but," a faint suggestion of cattiness crept into her voice "she has got rather a beaky nose . . . "

Andria did laugh then, quite without meaning to, a gurgle of real mirth coming up from deep inside her, and Constance laughed too.

"Oh, Con, you're *dreadful!*" Andria gasped, and suddenly the whole situation seemed hilariously funny . . .

Constance watched while Andria clutched her sides, laughing uncontrollably, tears running down her face.

"I'm glad you're amused, dear," she said tartly. "Let me inform you that I feel positively *deadly . . . *"

"Yes, you look it," Andria said bluntly. "Oh, I'm sorry, Con, but you must admit the thing has its funny side . . . and why should a prominent nose have anything to do with her not being a success in a film?"

"I don't think she'd be very photogenic," Constance explained, and Andria blew her nose and mopped her streaming eyes.

She picked up her cup, still grinning, and Constance said suddenly:

"I'm glad you can laugh, darling, after what's happened . . . I treated you very badly, didn't I? But when you told me you and Oliver weren't actually lovers it did seem to make the whole thing a little bit better . . . "

There was appeal in her amber eyes, and Andria said slowly:

"I don't think, looking back in hindsight, that Oliver ever *really* loved me, not like I loved him . . . "

"No," Constance said candidly. "I don't think he did, either, but that didn't make it any less painful for you. I am sorry, darling — have you forgiven us?"

For a moment the old hurt came back, raw and painful, then it subsided, and impulsively, Andria stretched out her hand and her mother took it, holding it tightly in hers.

"Oh, Andy, you are a pet," she said

huskily. "You're just like your father — he was a darling, too . . . Now what about you and Ellard? I take it you'll be getting married soon?"

"M'm," Andria nodded. "So hurry up and get well enough to come to the wedding, won't you? Now shall I have a look at this *rotten* script?"

She sat reading, becoming more engrossed by the minute, and Constance lay with her eyes closed, apparently satisfied that everything was in hand. Edith came in and took the tea tray away, and Andria hardly noticed her presence.

Finally she looked up, sighed, and said: "Crumbs," in an awed voice, and Constance giggled.

"I haven't heard you say that since you were a little girl," she commented. "It is a sticky one, isn't it?"

"Yes, it is, especially the end scene where the wretched woman breaks down and tells all," Andria said, laying the script down and stretching her arms above her head. "Honestly, Con, I don't know if I can do it — what do the other members of the cast think?"

"They're worried enough to try you

out," Constance said, fidgeting a little on her pillows. "And when Oliver talked to Ellard he agreed like a shot . . . By the way, darling, he won't know you're here, will he? Why don't you give him a ring now? He might be in his friend's flat at this time of day — so confusing, all these different times, aren't they? There's a phone in the hall, why don't you use that?"

"All right, I will," Andria stood up rather stiffly and went outside, wondering if she would be lucky enough to catch Ellard in. She had tried once before without success, and he had warned her that he would be very busy and it might be difficult to catch him at home.

She rang the number carefully, got a dialling tone, then nothing. Finally she hung up and went back to Constance, shrugging her shoulders.

"No luck?" Constance asked. She was cautiously sipping a glucose drink, but a little more colour had come into her cheeks and her eyes looked less heavy. "You will stay here tonight, won't you, Andy? There's plenty of room."

For a moment Andria almost agreed, then the thought of being under the same roof as Oliver made her pause. Was she really ready for that? Constance must have read her thoughts, because she said quickly:

"If you prefer it you can share a room with one of the girls in the play Oliver's in, she did offer . . . It might be better, in the circumstances. Will you wait till Oliver comes back and see him?"

"If it isn't necessary it might be wiser not to," Andria said frankly, and a wave of sheer thankfulness swept over her — at least she wouldn't be in the same play as Oliver, that would have been too much.

"All right, darling, the girl's address is Fourteen, Barton's Court, but I think you'd better wait until she gets back from the theatre and I'll give her a ring. Are you hungry? If you are Edith can cook you something."

"I am a bit," Andria admitted, and Constance reached for the bell again.

Edith appeared promptly, nodded at Constance's request, and looked sternly at Andria.

"Omelette do you?" she enquired, and Andria nodded.

"I think I might manage a *teeny* bit

of that," Constance said suddenly, and a sudden grim smile transformed Edith's face into something almost loving.

"Right," she said, and went, almost running.

"Poor Edith," Constance said ruefully. "I haven't eaten properly for over three weeks and she's been worried sick. So has Oliver. What's the time, darling? I think that girl might be home in about an hour, which just about gives you time to eat your supper. You'd better take that script with you. I'm sorry it's such an exacting part but that's the way things go, isn't it?"

It was, and suddenly Andria longed for Ellard in a way she'd never done before — longed for his physical presence, his ready grin, his strong arms round her — but Ellard was in New York, sorting out one mess, and it was up to Andria to help sort out another, if he was not to be in dreadful financial trouble. Could she do it?

"You'll be all right," Constance put her hand over Andria's. "Try and think of it as a challenge, and darling, if you make a success of it you really will be a name to reckon with in the theatre.

The omelette arrived, together with thin slices of bread and butter, and Andria was pleased to see that her mother did eat a little of it, and drink a glass of milk afterwards. Perhaps she thought that her part was being taken by someone reasonably competent had cheered her, or perhaps it was the feeling that she was once again on good terms with her daughter . . .

Later Constance rang the girl who had offered Andria her hospitality, and a few minutes later Andria was in a taxi, the script in her suitcase. She had surprised herself by hugging her mother hard before she left, to Edith's obvious approval, and Constance had returned the hug, breathing:

"Good luck, darling." into her ear.

"And," Andria thought grimly. "I'm going to need it."

Her new hostess was called Rosie, a dark, bubbly vivacious girl with an engaging smile. Andria liked her on sight, and fished out the script to show her while they had a cup of coffee together. Rosie read several pages with intense concentration, flicked through the rest of it, looked across at

Andria, and said: "Wow!" twice. Then she asked how Andria was going to play it.

"Straight, I suppose," Andria said. "There doesn't seem to be much scope for humour or light relief there, does there?"

"No, it's drama all the way through," Rosie said, running her hands through her abundant sooty curls. "But it's a peach of a part if you can get on top of it. I — I'll help you if I can."

"Thanks, Rosie, I'll probably need someone to hear my lines," Andria said gratefully. "But I don't think I'll try to learn anything tonight, I feel too tired."

"Yes, you must have had quite a day," Rosie commented, a careful note in her voice, and Andria wondered how much Oliver's acting colleagues actually knew about them, not that it mattered now.

"I hope your bed's comfortable," Rosie said, as they cleared away the coffee things. "I was lucky to find these rooms, I suppose, even if you can't move in the kitchen and the bathroom's shared."

Andria had not expected to sleep well that night, but she did, waking in the morning to find Rosie already up and frying bacon and eggs. She greeted Andria with a grin.

"I hope you're hungry," she said, as Andria reached for her dressing-gown. "I was starving. Come and sit down, you can wash afterwards."

Over breakfast they looked at the script again, Rosie making pertinent comments, and later that morning Andria sat down and concentrated on learning the first act, while Rosie went out to do some necessary shopping.

The play was the story of a woman who blindly adored her husband, innocently supposing that his money came from perfectly legitimate sources, who then discovered that it did not — the man she loved so passionately was a skilled and unscrupulous blackmailer, totally merciless to his victims, and morally responsible for the ruin of several of them and the suicide of two others.

Gradually the woman came to realise that her husband would be totally immune to appeals of any description, and that the only way to stop him would be to kill him . . .

Andria looked up from the script, shook herself mentally, and tried to think herself into the part, but it was difficult. Could you kill someone you really loved, whatever they'd done, and could you plot the killing as cold-bloodedly as the woman in the story?

Eventually she decided to go to the theatre and introduce herself to the other members of the cast, and set off in a taxi, not feeling at all confident.

The first person she saw as she went through the stage door was Michael Lester, and relief flooded through her.

"Oh, Michael!" she exclaimed, and his face lit up.

"Am I glad to see you, Andy!" He took her hands impulsively in his. "Got your script? What did you think of the play?"

"Terrific if you can manage the part," she said. "But Michael, I didn't realise you'd written this one as well — nobody told me."

"I'm beginning to wish I hadn't," Michael said frankly. "It's been nothing but trouble from start to finish . . . But come and meet the others, they'll want to get started. I'm acting as producer, by the way, and that's no rest cure, either."

He introduced her to the rest of the cast,

and apart from one woman who seemed to resent her presence, they were obviously relieved to see her, especially the girl who had taken over the part after Constance's understudy had left.

"It's been *awful,*" she blurted to Andria. "I knew I wasn't right for the part, but what could we do? The critics have given us a dreadful time — when do you think you'll be ready to take over?"

"Three days?" Andria suggested tentatively. "I've got to learn the lines, remember."

She sat in, listening in silence while Michael took the rest of them through a difficult scene he had not been happy with the day before, feeling more uneasy by the minute.

"I'm way out of my depth," she thought, and longed for Ellard again . . .

At Michael's suggestion she slipped into a seat amongst the matinée audience and watched the play, hoping it might clarify her jumbled thoughts, and as she sat there she began to realise that the woman she was to portray wasn't cold-blooded, she was shocked, disillusioned and desperate, and that was the way to play her.

The applause at the end of the performance was polite but not enthusiastic, and the theatre had only been half full. The play definitely needed a face lift, if it wasnt to close soon as a box-office failure.

"Well?" Michael asked, as Andria made her way back stage, and there was real appeal on his clever, sensitive face.

She smiled, trying to infuse her voice with confidence.

"I think I've got it, Michael," she said. "May I discuss it with you now?"

"Do you want the others as well?"

"Of course, it concerns them."

She found herself the focus of a very attentive circle, and as she tentatively outlined her idea, their expressions changed from near despair to dawning hope.

"It could work," Michael said, his voice lifting with his spirits. "That's what's been wrong, Andy — I made her too clinical . . . I'll have another look at the script, there might have to be a few alterations. Can everyone stay? Good."

9

IT was late when Andria got back to Rosie's flat, the amended script tucked under her arm. She let herself in quietly with the key Rosie had lent her, and flopped into a chair, closing her eyes. It had been a really hectic day. Michael had gone through the script line by line, making subtle alterations here and there, and then they had tried them out between the matinée and the evening performance.

"It's better, Michael," Andria said, and there were murmurs of agreement. "It's much better."

Now she had to learn her part, and learn it quickly, if more money wasn't to be lost, and the longing for Ellard swept over her again. Tired though she was, she *had* to get in touch, if only to tell him what had happened and let him know she was thinking about him.

There was a phone in the hall downstairs and she went down almost on tiptoe, hoping she wouldn't wake anyone up. She rang the number carefully, praying that this time she would get through, though of course there was no guarantee that Ellard would be there, anyway.

She waited, then there was a sharp little click, surprisingly clear, and a woman's voice said:

"Yes? Sheila here."

"Can I speak to Ellard, please?"

"I'm sorry, Ellard isn't here at the moment. Can I take a message?"

Andria hesitated, struggling with tiredness. It would take a long time to explain what had happened, and she wanted to speak to Ellard, not some strange woman.

"Could you tell him Andria called and that everything's all right, please?" she said finally, and a soft chuckle sounded on the other end of the line, deep and somehow — somehow sexy . . .

"So you're the new fiancée, are you?" Sheila said, and wide awake now, Andria stiffened to attention. "Ellard told me about you . . . how's the new play going?"

Andria hesitated, her thoughts whirling, while a strange ache gathered somewhere inside her. *Sheila* . . . Where had she heard that name before? It was definitely familiar . . .

"I think it will be better now," she said carefully. "Michael has made some changes."

"Right, I'll tell him." It sounded as though Sheila was smiling, the laugh was still in her voice. "Is there anything else?"

"I don't think so," Andria's hand went up to her forehead. "Would you — would you give him my love, please?"

"Oh, certainly. Goodbye."

Another click, and Andria knew that Sheila had hung up. She replaced the receiver herself, wondering why her hand was trembling, turned and went slowly upstairs. Who was Sheila and what was she doing in Ellard's flat? Then she remembered that it wasn't Ellard's flat, it was Anthony Segall's, so perhaps Sheila was a girl-friend of his, though she seemed to know a lot about Ellard.

Then she remembered, and the shock was so great that she almost fell up the last two stairs. Sheila was Ellard's former fiancée, the one who had jilted him to go to

181

New York, the one whose husband looked the other way when she had affairs . . .

Andria stumbled into the flat, closing the door mechanically behind her, her thoughts whirling, her knees shaking, and made her way to the nearest chair. She dropped into it, and sat staring into the darkness, willing herself to be calm, to think logically, to stop her heart from pounding its way out of her body. Just because Sheila was there it didn't mean that she and Ellard . . . he wasn't like that, and he'd said he was finished with Sheila, that their relationship was over long ago . . .

But if that was really so, *why* was Sheila there, and why was she answering the phone? Surely that indicated that she was well and truly at home there — you didn't answer other people's phones unless they asked you to . . .

Stop it, Andria told herself angrily, there could be a dozen logical explanations of Sheila's presence. Theatrical people knew each other, perhaps Sheila had simply come in to commiserate about the fire, perhaps she knew Anthony professionally, perhaps she'd simply met Ellard there and chatted to him as an old friend, in which case

Ellard would obviously have mentioned Andria to her.

"So you're the new fiancée, are you?"

There had been real amusement in her voice, as if the thought of Ellard engaged to be married was hilariously funny . . .

Well, maybe it was to her, she didn't hold marriage as in any way sacred, if Ellard was to be believed, and Andria felt sure he was.

"He'd have to be polite to her if she showed up, Andria thought. "He couldn't just ask her to leave . . . "

But if Ellard wasn't there, why was Sheila? Maybe she was there with Anthony . . . that must be it . . . Ellard couldn't, he wouldn't . . . or *could* he?"

Sitting with her aching head in her hands, Andria realised something that simply had not occurred to her before — Ellard was an extremely attractive man, other women must be drawn to him, and that he and Sheila had once been lovers . . .

"Dear God," Andria thought. "I'm *jealous* . . . I'm jealous of Ellard — I never thought I'd be jealous again, not after Oliver . . . "

183

And what did that mean? She would have said if anyone had asked her that she was very fond of Ellard, that she respected him as a person, that she would do her best to be a good wife to him, that she would have his children, but now she knew with a blinding rush of revelation that she felt far, far more than that — she loved Ellard, loved him even more than she had loved Oliver, and if he was unfaithful to her then she would surely die . . .

Tears started to run down her face, and she brushed them angrily away — crying was stupid, it got you nowhere, and what was she crying *about?* Two minutes stilted conversation on a long distance telephone? So Sheila had sounded amused, so what? It needn't necessarily *mean* anything . . .

And Ellard had written to her, short letters admittedly, but he had written, which surely he wouldn't have done if he had embarked on an affair with Sheila, and there wasn't an atom of proof that he had . . .

Andria got wearily to her feet, padded into the little bedroom she was sharing with Rosie, and started to undress in the dark so as not to disturb her. She crawled into bed, suddenly so exhausted that her eyes refused to stay open any longer, and was instantly asleep.

The next day she devoted herself entirely to learning her script, helped by Rosie, who proved to be nearly as much a tower of strength as Suky was. By the evening she had memorised the whole of the first act and part of the second, and she rang Michael Lester at the theatre and told him.

"Good," he said happily. "We tried it with the changes this afternoon, and even without you it went better. I think we might have a winner after all. Can you get the rest of it into your mind by tomorrow or is that too much to ask?"

"Could you give me the day after?"

"Yes, of course. Goodnight, Andy, and thanks."

She went back upstairs to the flat and cooked a meal, picked up the script, then put it down again. Even with her excellent memory there were limitations, and as Rosie pointed out, the mind didn't function well when you were very tired.

Better wait until tomorrow and start fresh then.

Rosie came back from the theatre and passed on a message from Oliver, keeping her tone casual and her back half turned.

"He said to tell you that Constance is a lot better," Rosie said. "The doctor says she can get up for a little while tomorrow."

"That's good," Andria said cheerfully, and suddenly saw that it was . . .

"How did your play go?" she asked, and Rosie smiled complacently.

"Very well," she said, grinning. "We're all pleased because that wretched fire must have cost Ellard and Michael thousands. Have you heard when he's coming home yet?"

"No, not yet, but then he may have written to the London flat," Andria kept her voice casual. "Suky will deal with that."

She had said nothing about Sheila to Rosie, just that she had got through to New York and left a message, which was true enough. She would have to learn to trust Ellard, and after what Oliver had done that wouldn't be easy.

Andria used all the concentration of which she was capable over the next two days, learning her lines and trying them out, mostly on Rosie, who displayed admirable patience.

"You'll be a wow, Andy," she said, as Andria shoved her script into a bag preparatory to leaving for the theatre on the third morning. "I wish I could be there."

"I wish you could, too," Andria smiled with lips that had suddenly become cold and stiff. "I'm going to need all the support I can get.

"Now you listen to me," Rosie said sternly, sounding rather like Suky. "You're a terrific actress, Andy — better than Constance if you want my opinion. You just get down to that theatre and save that play for Ellard."

"Right, I will," Andria grinned back, and Rosie said:

"Right, then," still sternly. Then she added:

"Good luck," and shooed Andria down the stairs.

Michael and the rest of the cast were waiting on stage for her, fidgeting a little,

187

and she knew that this was it — either this rehearsal would go with a swing or it would fall totally flat and they would be back where they'd started, with a monumental flop on their hands, the sort of disaster which loses thousands and does nobody any good, least of all the author and cast.

"I think I'm word perfect," she said, trying to sound confident.

"Right then, everybody," Michael said. "From the beginning."

Afterwards Andria couldn't remember at which point she had known it was going to be all right — perhaps halfway through the first act, when the heroine began to realise with dawning horror that she was married to a conscienceless sadist, or perhaps at the end when she knew she would have to kill him.

Michael stopped the play, took a long deep breath, and looked round at his cast. No one said anything for a moment, then someone said:

"Glory Alleluia!" in reverent tones, and a ripple of laughter suddenly released the tension like a cork coming out of a champagne bottle. Everyone began to talk at once, and Andria stood in their midst, so relieved that her knees felt weak.

"Coffee," Michael said firmly. "Then Act Two."

"You want me to go on this afternoon?" Andria asked, but she knew the answer already.

"You bet your sweet life we do," Michael said, smiling at last. "We're going to give this thing our damnedest and make those *vultures* eat their reviews! *And* I hope it chokes them!"

Someone asked if Michael had thought to notify the Press that Andria was taking over the part, and he nodded.

"That ought to fetch them in," he said grimly. "Right, Act Two, everybody, and give it all you've got."

Michael insisted on taking Andria out for a quick lunch before the afternoon performance, and he talked about everything but the play. His wife was in the same boat as Constance, he said, pregnant but very well, except that she was worried about what had happened and would be relieved to see Ellard back again.

"So shall I," Andria thought ruefully, and the sickening doubt swept over her again, making her put down her knife and fork and clasp her hands in her lap to disguise their sudden trembling.

Michael ordered coffee, then glanced at the clock, which seemed to Andria to be remorsely ticking away the minutes to her triumph or doom — it would be one or the other, and frankly she wasn't at all sure which.

"We'd better get back," Michael said, easing his long thin length off the chair. "All right, Andy?"

"M'm," she nodded, thinking it was rather like going to the dentist, only ten times worse. "I suppose this is it, Michael."

"We'll soon know," he said, as they stepped into the sunshine. "But I'm not worried about you, not at all . . . "

There was real expectancy backstage, and as Andria got into her stage clothes and made up she wondered if the critics had indeed arrived, and what they would think of her. Her face in the mirror looked deadly pale and to her critical view almost gaunt, and when someone tapped on the door she started wildly and swung round in her seat.

"Come in," she called, and even her voice sounded strange, husky and uneven.

"It's flowers for you, Andria."

"Oh! Oh, thank you."

The girl laid the bouquet in her lap, smiled and went, and Andria stared down at them for a moment, her heart thumping inside her. Could they be from Ellard? She looked at the pretty little card.

"Good luck, darling. Con and Oliver" it said, and for a moment she felt sickeningly disappointed.

Then her common sense reasserted itself. Ellard couldn't know exactly when she was starting to play the part, there hadn't been time to let him know, so how could he send her flowers?

But Con and Oliver had remembered, and unexpectedly she warmed to them — they wanted her to succeed, as much for her own sake as Ellard's, and her resolve stiffened. This afternoon she would show everyone what she was capable of, or die in the attempt . . .

Someone called "Five minutes, Miss Vincent," and she got up, shook herself mentally, and walked firmly out of the dressing-room and into the wings.

The first act was difficult. During the first ten minutes she had to portray a woman bubbling with happiness, totally contented with her life, and then — gradually — equally total disillusionment setting in, followed by sheer horror . . .

The audience was quiet, there was no fidgeting or coughing, none of the signs of boredom, but an intense absorbed interest. Andria sensed it even while she concentrated on her role, and dimly realised that this was better, much better . . . Almost before she knew it the curtain sank down, the applause crashed out, and Michael hurried on to the stage, beaming, and hugged her until she was breathless.

"Great, wonderful, everybody!" he exclaimed. "That's given them something to talk about."

"Are the critics there?" she asked as they left the stage, and Michael nodded.

"Yes, including that one your mother can't stand — what's his name?"

"I don't care, so long as he gives us a decent review," Andria said, as the scene shifters hurried on stage. "It is better, isn't it?"

"It's a different play," someone assured

192

her, and she went into her dressing-room to change, reassured. Perhaps they had pulled it off, after all . . .

The curtain rose on the second act, and the audience hushed as Andria set the scene for the murder she was about to carry out, moving like an automaton but with a deadly purpose. There was total and absolute silence during the whole act, then thunderous applause, and one of the actors wiped his brow and heaved a long sigh of relief.

"One more to go," he said, and to Andria it sounded like the last hurdle in a hard difficult race.

Afterwards she found it difficult to remember exactly how the last act went, but she did remember the applause and the curtain calls. They went on and on, the audience on its feet, some of them shouting, and Michael, a delirious smile on his face, said:

"We've done it, folks, it's OK."

It seemed like an understatement, but the relief was so great that Andria's knees flowed like water as she finally went back to her dressing-room, and she collapsed into a chair and leaned back, closing her eyes. It was over, at least for a few hours, and it had gone well — that was all that mattered . . .

A few minutes later Michael tapped on the door and said that he had phoned Ellard, but without success.

"Pity, I'd have liked to have spoken to him," he said, and Andria nodded.

"So would I," she said feelingly under her breath, and Michael shot her a surprised, rather perplexed glance.

"Anything wrong, Andy?" he asked, and she forced a quick smile.

"No, not really," she said, keeping her tone light. "It's just that every time I try either he's not there or somebody else answers. Maybe we should telex him, or I could write again."

"He has written to you?" Michael asked, and she nodded.

"I — I do miss him, Michael," she said, and to her astonishment he took her hand and held it tightly for a moment.

"So do I, we all do," he said, and she had the surprising thought that Michael had somehow sensed her uneasiness, although she had said nothing. "He's very missable, is Ellard."

Then, equally suddenly, Michael became brisk and sensible.

"Now you go on home and have some tea and a rest," he said. "That performance must have really taken it out of you, and you must be fresh for tonight. I'll get you a taxi. No, don't argue, there's a good girl, the producer knows best, even if he is only a stand-in one. See you tonight."

Rosie's little flat felt like a haven of rest and peace, and Andria flung all the windows open to let in the late afternoon sunlight, wishing she felt more elated. Goodness knows she had cause to be thankful — everything pointed to a theatrical success, and her own career would receive a tremendous boost if it was. But it felt like nothing against this horrible feeling that she might be losing Ellard, and losing him to someone like Sheila, who hadn't, Andria thought cattily, the morals of a backyard cat . . .

But Ellard would know that, he'd said it himself, so why couldn't she trust him? *Why* be so convinced he was betraying her with Sheila, on the strength of one silly phone call? It must be something to do with the sickening shock she had

195

received over Oliver and Constance, which had shaken her to the depths of her being . . . But Ellard wasn't Oliver, he was a different man, someone with real standards in every respect, not just *morally* . . .

Andria put the kettle on, giving herself a mental shake. Ellard would be home soon, with a perfectly normal explanation, and all this heartache would be proved totally pointless. She had to believe that . . .

The evening performance of the play was a repeat of the matinée, and afterwards Michael took the entire cast out to dinner to celebrate what he called "our little miracle".

"There'll be some different sort of reviews in the Press tomorrow," he said with quiet satisfaction. "I'll try and get a message to Ellard when I know what the critics have actually said."

The next morning Andria found out. Rosie went out early for the papers, and when they turned to the entertainments pages they found almost rave reviews. "A miraculous transformation", one critic had written. "Andria Vincent is superb". "This *must* be seen", someone else insisted. "An incredible performance from a girl not yet twenty."

"Told you so," Rosie said smugly. "I knew you could do it."

"I'm just glad it's come right for Ellard and Michael," Andria said, picking up another paper. I was worried, Rosie — everything seemed to be going wrong at once."

"It happens like that sometimes," Rosie said wisely. "Then when it starts going right, everything goes right — haven't you noticed that yourself?"

"M'm," Andria nodded. "I'd like to phone Ellard, but it's still night in New York so I'll have to wait."

She filled in the morning writing letters, one to Suky and a quick one to Constance, more to avoid calling on her again and risking meeting Oliver. It was stupid, she acknowledged that to herself, but she didn't want to see him just yet, and yet she knew she would have to sooner or later. Then she wrote to the cast of the play in London, telling them all was well and wishing her understudy continuing success. She slipped out to post them, then came back, and as she pushed open the door and glanced at her watch she knew that it was time to phone Ellard and that she was almost too apprehensive to do it . . .

Suppose — suppose that Sheila was still there? Wouldn't that prove conclusively that there was something going on? Was it better to know or not know? She hesitated, took a deep breath, and picked up the phone. After a pause the ringing started, and Andria waited, her mouth dry and her hands damp, until it became apparent that nobody was going to answer. Not knowing whether to be disappointed or relieved she hung up, then forced herself to go inside the flat and help Rosie with a quick, light lunch for them both, consoling herself with the fact that if Ellard wasn't at home then neither was Sheila . . .

This time the theatre was packed, unusually so for a matinée, and Michael told her that the bookings were coming in fast and furious.

"For months ahead," he said with visible relief, and she realised suddenly how traumatic it must have been for him to find himself in charge of a production which was going badly wrong at the worst possible time.

"Thanks to you, Michael," Andria said impulsively, and he looked at her and smiled.

"As to that, opinions differ," he said gravely. "But it's a success and that's all that matters. Did you manage to contact Ellard, by the way?"

"I tried but he wasn't there," Andria said, keeping her tone matter-of-fact. "I wish I knew when he was coming back."

"Soon I should imagine," Michael said. "Can't be soon enough for me . . . right, Andy, time to get ready."

She went to her dressing-room, wondering if Michael was right and Ellard was coming home quickly. Suddenly she longed for him with an intensity she hadn't felt before — longed to be assured of his love and his loyalty, longed to see his smile, to feel his arms round her . . . She gave a long ragged sigh and picked up her lipstick.

The matinée concluded to prolonged and enthusiastic applause, the curtain calls over, Andria went back to her dressing-room while the rest of the chattering cast returned to theirs. She was beginning to feel more at home in the part, more competent to play it, and as she pushed open the dressing-room door she had a feeling of sudden satisfaction at the way things had gone.

Then she stood still in the doorway, her eyes widening in total surprise as Oliver got up from the chair he'd been perched on and greeted her with a smile.

"Hello, Andy, long time no see," he said, holding out his hand. "Hope you don't mind my waiting for you. I've seen the show, we didn't have a matinée today so I thought I'd come along and watch, then I could report back to Con."

She took his hand with a little smile, and to her faint surprise his touch did absolutely nothing to her — nothing fluttered inside her, nothing thumped — it might have been any man's warm well-shaped hand she was holding, and she released it with another smile.

"What did you think?" she asked, and Oliver looked intently at her for a moment without speaking.

"I think," he said slowly and deliberately. "that you are probably the best young dramatic actress to hit the theatrical scene for about ten years. You were super, Andy, just as Con and I knew you would be. A great performance, really terrific. If anything you were better than Con would have been in the part."

"Well, thank you," she was genuinely touched. "That — that's very kind of you, Oliver, I really treasure that."

"It's true. Con will be delighted."

"You'd better not say I'm better than she would have been," Andria said mischievously, and Oliver flung back his head and roared with laughter.

Then, abruptly, he stopped.

"Know something, Andy?" he said slowly. "I don't think she'd give a damn if I did."

"No, you're right," Andria said. "Con's got a lot of faults, but she — she's not mean and she's never been jealous."

"Pointless sort of emotion, jealousy," Oliver said seriously.

"Yes, it is," Andria agreed soberly, and he gave her a quick, frowning glance.

"Is everything OK, Andy?" he asked. "Apart from the play, I mean."

"I — I'm missing Ellard," she told him, and he looked at her again, his frown deepening.

"He'll be back, pet," he said gently, sounding Andria thought rather like an affectionate elder brother. "Before very long, I should think."

"Can't be too soon for me," Andria said, but her light tone didn't sound quite right, even in her own ears.

"Something," Oliver said bluntly, and she remembered that he used to be able to read her like a book. "Is up. What is it? Maybe I can help."

The need to talk to someone overcame her, and she stared almost imploringly at him.

"You won't say anything to anyone, not even Con?"

"Not even Con. Cross my heart and hope to be booed off the stage."

"It — it's Sheila . . . "

It was a tremendous relief to tell him, her hand in his, and he sat quietly listening, not interrupting until she faltered to the end of her story.

"M'm," he said, after a pause. "Not much to go on there, Andy . . . Do you know what I think? I think Sheila just called on Anthony to say she was sorry about the fire, and Ellard happened to be

202

there. Naturally they would talk but I'm damned sure that's all they did do."

"Then why was she there answering the phone?" Andria asked. "She was either there alone or she was lying and someone else was there, and Oliver, I keep telling myself it wasn't Ellard but the — the thought just won't go away . . ."

"It's far more likely to have been Anthony if someone else was with her," Oliver said calmly. "After all, it is his flat, and he could have asked her to answer the phone if he was busy with something else."

"I suppose so." Andria gave a wobbly smile. "You're right, of course you are . . ."

"It's not like you to be suspicious of people," Oliver said, his eyes searching her face, a slight frown between his brows. "Snap out of it, Andy — Ellard loves you, I'm absolutely sure of that — he finished with Sheila years ago, and he's got too much discernment to start anything with her after all this time. He'll have too much else on his mind for one thing."

He smiled, and his bracing tone had the right effect — suddenly her suspicions seemed stupid, and she smiled back, more naturally this time.

"That's better," Oliver said. "That's more like the Andy I know. I'll have a bet with you. Ellard will be back within the week and if you mention Sheila he'll probably have difficulty in remembering just when he saw her and what he said."

He kissed her quickly and left with a wave of the hand, and Andria drew a wavering breath. Oliver had reassured her to a certain extent, and his advice had been plain common sense. Forget Sheila and get on with what had to be got on with . . .

Two more days passed, and the play seemed to go from strength to strength as Andria and the other actors worked themselves into their parts, and they played to packed houses and further acclaim from the critics. Suky and Bill appeared unexpectedly, having managed to get enough time off to do it together, and were introduced to everyone backstage before they hurriedly left again. Even seeing Suky for such a short space of time raised Andria's spirits, and the next night her mother came, looking pale but better, and sat through the performance with Edith beside her like an attendant dragon. She came into Andria's dressing-room afterwards and looked at her daughter almost with awe.

"Well, I knew you'd do it well," she commented quietly. "But I didn't know just *how* well. Andy, I'm tremendously proud of you."

"Thanks," Andria mumbled, suddenly embarrassed. "But you'd have done it every bit as well if you'd been all right."

"I don't think so," Constance shook her head with endearing honesty. "No, darling, you've made the part your own — Ellard's going to be absolutely thrilled when he sees you. Have you heard from him?"

"Not recently, but everyone seems to think he'll be back soon," Andria said, wondering if her mother would detect something wrong from her carefully bright tone. "I hope so."

"M'm," Constance nodded, her brilliant eyes searching Andria's face. "So do I. Right, darling, I must go — the doctor only let me off the leash on condition I came away straight after the performance. Edith, can you get a taxi, please?"

Edith vanished, and Constance eyed Andy again.

"Anything wrong, pet?" she asked, and Andria quickly shook her head.

"Just a bit tired, that's all," she replied, and Constance nodded.

"Well, after that you're entitled to be," she said. "Take care of yourself, Andy — Ellard *needs* you for this, you know."

She kissed Andria and went, and Andria thought forlornly that she needed Ellard, and needed him desperately, needed to *know* that he still loved her — she would not, could not be happy again until then . . .

10

ANDRIA may have agreed with Oliver that jealousy was a pointless emotion, but during the next few days she discovered that it was a very difficult one to fight. Try as she would to believe in Ellard, little poisonous thoughts like the creeping tendrils of some noxious plant kept coming to her, making her literally grit her teeth and shake herself to combat them. Useless to tell herself it was all nonsense — the thoughts came back, and the situation wasn't helped by the fact that she heard nothing at all from Ellard.

Finally in desperation she sank her pride and phoned Suky.

"I just wondered if there was a letter — letters for me, she said tentatively, and Suky, sounding surprised, said there wasn't.

"I'll send anything on if it comes," she promised. "Andy, is everything all right? You sound a bit strange."

"Just — just rather tired," Andria said,

subduing a longing to tell Suky everything. "Sorry I bothered you, Suky — hope I didn't get you out of bed."

"That's all right," Suky suppressed a yawn. "Andy, you will be able to get to our wedding, won't you? It just occurred to me that it might be difficult for you but I'd hate you to miss it."

"Don't worry, I won't," Andria promised firmly. "I'm your bridesmaid, remember?"

Suky laughed, said goodbye and hung up, and after a moment Andria did the same. No letters . . . A faint forlorn hope died inside her. Whatever anyone liked to say, she should have heard *something* . . . Ellard should have written, or at least phoned. Unless of course he was otherwise engaged . . .

"And with that awful Sheila," Andria thought, and tramped disconsolately back upstairs.

When Michael showed her another review she had to make a conscious effort to smile and look pleased.

"'This production goes from strength to strength'," Michael quoted, beaming round complacently at the cast. "I have the feeling Ellard will want to take this to London soon.

There were smiles and nods all round, but Andria had to turn away as stupid tears dimmed her eyes. None of this seemed real to her — the only reality was Ellard and the intensity of her feelings for him . . .

"If only I'd been more — more positive, let him know how I really felt, or was beginning to feel," she thought miserably. "Instead of just — just being passive and affectionate . . . "

But passive wasn't the right word either, and feeling the beginnings of a headache gathering in her temples, she swallowed hard and nodded agreement with the others.

Then someone asked the question sheer pride had kept Andria from asking.

"Have you heard anything from him?"

"No," Michael shook his head. "Not for a few days now, but he'll be back soon, so let's keep the production up to standard, shall we? Right, people, time to change."

There was something to be said for both matinees and evening performances, Andria decided as she went into the now familiar dressing-room, they kept you from thinking too much. Having to concentrate so hard on a difficult role tended to block out other more troubling faults, and it was almost with relief that she heard the call for beginners and walked into the wings for her first entrance.

As usual the play took over, and as the applause crashed out at the end of the first act she knew their success was continuing, and smiled a wry little smile, wishing she could feel better pleased. She went back to the dressing-room and sat quietly waiting for the next act and gathering up her resources, her eyes closed and her mind a deliberate blank.

And then, the next morning, there on the mat was the letter she had been waiting for — air mail and with an American stamp. She snatched it up and held it to her cheek, then ran upstairs with it clutched in her hand, glad that Rosie had gone out early and she could read Ellard's message in peace and privacy.

It was quite short.

"Andy darling,

"Sorry I haven't written before, I tried to get you on the phone but somehow I missed you. Things are getting straight here at last so I'll be back soon.

"I hear you're doing marvels with Con's

part, but then I knew you would. When I get back there's something important I want to talk about.

"See you.

"Love,

"Ellard."

So he had tried to phone her, Andria thought, and her spirits rose. It was easy to choose the wrong time, especially with the few hours difference, and he was coming back — soon, he said . . .

She read the letter again, hanging over every word, and wishing the letter was ten times as long. What was the important something he wanted to discuss? Another play? A trip to New York later that year? He had mentioned that before.

Or was it — could it be something else? Something about himself and *Sheila?*

"Don't be a fool," she told herself angrily. "Why should it be? He sent his love, didn't he . . . "

She slipped the brief letter into her handbag, pushed the doubting thought away, and went on with tidying up the flat. Rosie came back laden with shopping, and grinned when Andria told her about the short letter.

"Ellard always was a man of few words," she said, dumping her bag on the table with a bump. "But so long as he's OK and he's coming back. There must have been a lot to do, Andy — the fire insurance people would want to know exactly what caused the fire and so on, and they can be awfully sticky about things like that even if it's just a house fire. We had one at home once and it took months to settle."

"I suppose so," Andria said, feeling comforted. "It's just that it seems so far away, somehow . . . "

"I know, Rosie said, and an unexpected blush crept into her cheeks. "I've got a fellow, but he's in Australia. He's coming back soon but sometimes I worry in case he's — well, in case he's met another girl. Maybe he worries in case I've met another guy!"

Andria laughed, Rosie grinned again, and things moved a little more into perspective. Was Rosie right? Could Ellard be worrying in case she had got another fellow? Somehow Andria didn't think so, but Ellard had been bitterly hurt once himself . . . Which brought them back to Sheila again!

"I must stop this," Andria thought,

and asked Rosie what they should have for lunch.

She was late for the theatre that evening and only had time to notice that the auditorium was even more crammed than usual before it was time to go and change, and then the play swept her away again. Once more engulfed in the part she played it with all her might, and once again the applause was sustained and enthusiastic.

Backstage at the end of the first act she shook herself into reality, exchanged smiling remarks with the other actors, and pushed open the door of her dressing-room. Then she stopped dead, her mouth falling open in sheer incredulous wonder. The room was a sea of flowers — roses, lilies, carnations almost fell over each other in scented abandon, and as her eyes travelled slowly round the room she wondered, dazed, where all this had come from.

Then she saw a small white envelope lying on her dressing-table, and with trembling fingers she picked it up and took out the card inside.

"Love from Ellard," it said. "See you after the performance.

For a moment she failed to grasp the significance of this, then with a rush of joy she realised that he was back, that he was here, maybe actually in the theatre somewhere, though she hadn't seen him.

She stood still amongst the blossoms, the little card pressed to her cheek, tears cascading down her face. He was back, he was home, he'd sent his love . . . Suddenly the world was a glowing, wonderful place, it was heavenly to be alive, to be herself, to be waiting for her lover . . .

"Five minutes, Miss Vincent."

She jerked back to attention and began to change quickly, her breathing quick and hurried. No, that wouldn't do, this was the second act, quite crucial to the story — she must be calm and controlled, it would be fatal to forget her lines or make one wrong movement now . . .

She took a deep, steadying breath, inspected her make-up, and walked steadily out of the dressing-room, concentrating on her opening lines. All those flowers . . . She'd never seen so many, not even in Constance's dressing-room . . .

The curtain rose, the audience hushed, and Andria made her entrance, the murder weapon concealed in the folds of her skirt. If Ellard was watching somewhere, she thought, he was going to see something worth coming home for . . .

She had half hoped he would be waiting in her dressing-room at the end of the second act, but he wasn't, and she forced back her disappointment. He had said "after the performance" so maybe he was still travelling. He might even meet her outside the theatre, she would have to be patient until then.

She looked round at the flowers, changed, repaired her make-up, sat still for a few minutes with her eyes closed, then got up and walked into the wings, willing herself to give another good performance.

Judging by the tumultuous applause at the end of the play she accomplished it, and as the cast took its fifth curtain call Andria looked quickly round the theatre, her glance flicking from face to face. She couldn't see Ellard, but that didn't mean anything. In a full house like this it was often impossible to pick out one single person however hard you tried.

The audience let them go eventually,

and as the curtain went down Andria gave a long sigh of sheer relief. Michael came up to her, taking her arm and steering her into a quiet corner.

"Andy, Ellard's back, as I guess you know already," he said. "He isn't alone, he's got someone with him — they'll be coming back stage in a minute. Do you want to go and freshen up?"

Oh, my God, Andria thought, *Sheila* . . .

"Yes," she said in a voice she didn't recognise as her own. "Yes, I do, Michael . . . I'll go . . . "

She never knew how she reached her dressing-room without collapsing in the passage, but she accomplished it somehow and staggered to her chair, her knees shaking and her face lint white under her make-up. Ellard had brought Sheila back with him . . . But *why?* Surely not just to torture her . . . there must be another reason . . .

Someone tapped on the door, she turned slowly in her seat, and forced her stiff lips to say, "Come in."

The door opened and Ellard appeared. Andria had just time to notice that he was wearing a new suit and a carnation in his lapel, then he was striding across the room and gathering her fiercely into his arms.

"Oh, Andy, Andy," he whispered in her ear. "I've missed you so much — you don't know how much . . . "

His lips found hers in an eager embrace, and Andria, her senses swimming, kissed him back.

They clung together, Ellard hugging her until she gasped for breath, then he released her reluctantly, grinned, and said quietly:

"There's someone you *must* meet, Andy — wait, I'll call him."

Him — it wasn't Sheila! Weak with shock and relief, she smiled mistily up at Ellard, who moved to the door, opened it and called:

"In here, Cy."

A round little man appeared in the doorway, a fat cigar in one hand, and Andria thought:

"He looks exactly like a film producer or something like that."

She rose unsteadily to her feet, holding out her hand as Ellard introduced them, and Cy took it, beaming.

"So you're the little lady Ellard's been telling me all about," he said. "I saw your performance tonight, what a triumph!"

He turned to Ellard, the beam disappearing, suddenly serious.

"You're right," he said. "It would make a great film. Can we get the rest of the cast together and talk about it?"

"You want to film the play?" Andria gasped, and Cy nodded.

"That's the idea," he said. "It's a great idea and a great script. Ellard, can you get out there and stop everyone from leaving?"

Ellard vanished, and Andria stood staring at Cy, not knowing what to say. No wonder Ellard had been busy! She wondered where he had met Cy — what was his other name? Ellard had said it but in her bewildered state she had forgotten it already . . .

"I — I've never been in a film before," she said, and Cy grinned.

"There's a first time for everything, Andy," he said. "I think you'll be a natural."

"I hope so," she was beginning to feel less shocked. "But — but Cy, there's a wedding I *must* go to first."

"Yes, I know, your friend Suky," Cy said unexpectedly. "Ellard told me. Sure you can go . . . and isn't there another wedding you ought to get settled right away?"

His eyes, shrewd and kindly, searched her face, and she felt a blush rising in her cheeks, and nodded shyly.

"Make it soon," Cy said. "That boy's crazy about you, but I guess you know that already."

Andria was saved from replying by Ellard re-appearing in the doorway.

"Everyone's backstage, Cy," he said. "And pretty excited."

"Right," Cy said, and trundled purposefully out of the dressing-room, leaving Ellard and Andria to follow more slowly.

He tucked her hand into his arm, smiling down at her.

"I was so proud of you tonight," he said softly. "We were in the audience all the time, Andy, but I didn't come backstage because I didn't want to break your concentration. Shall we go and listen to what Cy proposes? It'll be good whatever it is, he's a first-class producer."

"I — I'm sure he is," Andria said. "It's

just a bit difficult to take it all in, that's all."

"It's been a pretty hectic time for you, hasn't it?" he remarked thoughtfully. "How is Con, by the way? I had a word with Oliver a couple of days back and he said she was improving."

"She's been to see the show," Andria said. "She — she was very nice about my performance.

"So she should be," Ellard said drily. "Come on, Andy, we don't want to miss Cy's briefing."

He was standing on a wooden box in the centre of the stage, the cast clustered round him, explaining his proposals and waving his hands to emphasise a point to his dazed-looking audience. As Andria's gaze travelled from face to face, she couldn't help remembering the dispirited people she had first met only a fortnight or so ago, and she marvelled how things could change so completely in such a short space of time.

She stood side by side with Ellard, his arm round her, his shoulder pressed against hers, feeling his warmth, and the ghost of Sheila vanished as if it had never been.

Andria would have liked the rest of the evening alone with Ellard, but Cy insisted on the whole cast coming to dinner with him, and Ellard went off to phone for bookings, coming back a little later to say that he had managed to get them all in at the same place but they had better leave at once.

"Great," Cy beamed. "OK, folks, let's go. Did you ring for taxis as well, Ellard?"

"I did," Ellard grinned back. "It'll be a bit of a squash but we can just about do it."

Andria had to sit on Ellard's lap, hemmed in by Cy and her own understudy, who had apparently been crying with happiness, but somehow nobody minded. They spilled out on the pavement outside the restaurant, Andria still clinging to Ellard's hand, and Cy shepherded them all inside, still grinning happily.

"He seems so sure it will be a real success," Andria whispered, and Ellard nodded.

"Just look at Michael, have you ever seen him so excited?" he whispered back, and Andria shook her head.

"It's marvellous for him," she said, as

they went through the swing doors. "I bet he can't wait to get away to tell Polly."

It was almost one o'clock when the dinner party finally broke up, and Andria, standing outside once more with Ellard, wondered dreamily where he was staying that night.

"I've booked into the same hotel as Cy," he said, as if he read her thoughts. "How tired are you, Andy? Too tired to come and talk for a bit? Or would you rather leave it till the morning?"

"I'd like to talk." She tucked her hand into his arm, feeling the hard muscle under the fine material of his sleeve. "Would the lounge be private enough?"

"I shouldn't think there'd be many guests around at this hour," Ellard said, smiling briefly. "If it wasn't such a superior sort of place I'd suggest my room, but it could be embarrassing if anyone saw us. Shall we share a taxi with Cy?"

"M'm," she nodded as one appeared round the corner and Ellard hailed it.

Snuggled in the corner with her head pillowed on Ellard's shoulder she almost fell asleep, but she roused as the taxi drew up outside an imposing well-lit portico.

As they went up the wide marble steps she thought that Cy certainly believed in doing things in style.

Cy said goodnight in the foyer, treating them to a knowing wink before he trudged up the curving stairs, and a quick jaunty wave as he vanished from sight.

"He's a great little guy," Ellard said, his arm round Andria's shoulders. "Come in here, darling, and sit down."

The lounge was as impressive as the rest of the building, but Ellard led the way to a dimly lit corner and Andria sank down into a well-cushioned settee.

"Sorry I can't offer you a drink, the bar's closed," Ellard said as he joined her.

"Doesn't matter," Andria curled up beside him and they exchanged a long, slow kiss. "I want to know all about *everything . . .* "

"Right, where shall I start?" Ellard paused as if to gather his thoughts.

"The beginning might be a good idea," Andria suggested saucily, and he bit her ear gently by way of punishment.

"Well, when I got to New York I went straight round to the hospital to see Anthony. He was obviously shocked but not too bad physically, except that he had some nasty burns on his right hand where he'd tried to drag a lump of burning debris out of the way, and he was worried sick over the insurance."

"Was there any trouble?" Andria asked.

"It took the forensic people a long time to establish the cause of the fire, but eventually they traced it to a smouldering cigarette, and we were covered for that," Ellard said. "The insurance people decided there wasn't any negligence on our part so we'll get our money, thank goodness. God knows what we'd have done if they'd decided we were liable."

"That would have been awful," Andria agreed. "So what happened after that?"

"Anthony was allowed home and we worked from his apartment. It took a lot of phone calls and letters to get everything settled and one of our actors — bless his kind heart — slapped a writ on us for loss of livelihood, just to make things a bit better. We had to pay them all off and that didn't help at all."

"Are you — are you solvent now?" Andria asked hesitantly, and Ellard nodded.

"Just about, and rebuilding," he said. "It should be finished in about three months, then we can reopen. Anthony's working on a new play to celebrate the occasion. We were going to suggest you as the leading lady, but then I heard about Con and you stepped into the breach."

His arm tightened round her.

"I can't tell you what a relief that was," he said. "We'd really have been in trouble if the play had folded on top of everything else. You were wonderful, Andy, I don't know how you got it all together in the time."

"I never thought I would," she confessed. "Rosie helped me with the lines, and Michael made some alterations to the script. Honestly I think it would have flopped if he hadn't.

"I think it would, too," Ellard agreed, and a little silence fell.

Then Ellard gave a sudden, unexpected chuckle.

"How did Con take the idea of being a mother?" he asked, and Andria began to giggle almost uncontrollably as she remembered the scene in her mother's bedroom.

She described it to Ellard, who laughed in his turn, then became serious again.

225

"So — so are you cured of Oliver now?" he asked, his eyes searching her face.

"Cured completely," she said quietly and honestly. "He came to see me after I took over and said they were both — well, you can guess — and it was just like talking to a nice elder brother, nothing more."

She sensed rather than felt tension going out of Ellard, and with a shock realised that he had not been as sure of her as he would have wanted to be — and then, in that moment, she remembered Sheila . . .

"Ellard," she said. "There — there's something I want to ask you, and I hope you don't mind."

"What is it?" he asked.

"I — I tried to phone you at Anthony's flat. I got through but he didn't answer it, a girl did and she said it was Sheila. I — I wondered what she was doing there."

Ellard looked at her for a moment, then a delighted smile spread across his face.

"Don't tell me you were *jealous?*" he exclaimed.

"Not at all," she said with dignity. "I just *wondered . . .* "

He looked quizzically at her, his head on one side.

"Oh, all right then, I was! I was *sick* with jealousy, if you want to know!" she exclaimed angrily. "I couldn't get it out of my mind, especially after you told me what she was like with men. Then she said you weren't there, but you'd told her about us, and it sounded as if she was having a jolly good laugh about the whole thing! So I wondered . . . "

"Oh, darling, I — I'm sorry." There was a suspicious tremor in Ellard's voice as if he was struggling with laughter himself. "If I'd only realised . . . Listen, pet, what happened was this. Sheila heard about the fire, of course, and came round to Anthony's flat to see how he was. They knew each other because she was once in a film he'd written some of the script for, and they were friends. No more than that, I think, but I didn't ask. I happened to be there at the time, and for sheer politeness sake I had to talk to her, and I told her about you.

"She congratulated me and then I went out, leaving her alone with Anthony. What happened after that I don't know, but I think I can guess what happened about the phone. Anthony's hand was still heavily bandaged, and he's one of these people who's very right-handed and finds it very difficult to do anything much with his left. He probably asked her to take the call and she did."

"As simple as that?" Andria looked imploringly at him, and he nodded.

"As simple as that," he said. "She was gone when I got back to the apartment and I didn't see her again. Nor," he added firmly "did I have the least desire to do so. I don't particularly like the sort of woman Sheila has grown into, though I must admit she's a superb actress and very attractive. Her wretched husband must think so too or he'd never put up with her antics."

Relief flooded through Andria like a cleansing tide, and she closed her eyes momentarily.

"I thought — Ellard, I'm a fool — but I thought when Michael said you'd got someone with you — I thought it was *Sheila* . . . "

"Never in a thousand years," Ellard said drily, capturing both Andria's hands in his. "I've got some instinct for self-preservation left. And darling, I love *you* . . . "

"I love you, too," Andria said huskily.

"I didn't know how much until you'd gone and I heard Sheila answering your phone. I didn't know I could feel so shattered — it was worse than when Oliver . . . "

Her voice broke and Ellard pulled her closely into his arms.

"My darling girl," he whispered in her ear. "Sheila means absolutely nothing to me now, that's all over and finished years ago. It's you I want, and I want you for good, for always and ever — understand?"

"M'm," she nodded, still choking on her tears. "I feel the same about you, Ellard — I don't ever want to be parted from you again."

Another guest, late in from some function, walked through the room, and they drew reluctantly apart, Andria dabbing her wet face with the handkerchief Ellard thrust into her hand.

As soon as the man had gone Andria asked what she had been meaning to ask before, and Ellard laughed.

"How did I meet Cy? Well, once again he knew Anthony, who'd done the odd script for him, and he came round to see how Anthony was. As a matter of fact we had a whole procession of Anthony's friends in and out of the apartment all the time, which didn't help with the paper work and phoning at all.

"Cy and I got talking and I told him about you taking over the part from your mother, and so on, and he seemed interested, so Anthony suggested he flew over with me and saw the play. He's got other business here so he agreed at once, and here he is."

"He said we ought to get married soon," Andria said, wriggling back into Ellard's embrace, and his arms tightened round her again.

"I couldn't agree more," he said. "Listen, darling, I've been thinking — you'll have to keep on with your part for a few weeks, at least until we find someone else who can take over, or put on something else. Frankly I wanted to take the show to London, not film it, but obviously it's a terrific opportunity and we can't let it go, for Michael's sake if nothing else. So suppose I found us a small flat for the time being while we settled things here?"

"That would be wonderful," Andria said. "Then we'll be around for Suky's wedding. When does Cy want to start filming?"

"In the autumn I believe," Ellard smiled. "So it all fits in very well. Autumn in California must be rather nice."

"Anywhere with you would be nice," Andria said.

"Right, that's settled, then. Now about that wedding. Andy, would you mind something quiet in a registry office? We could fix it up quickly, or do you want a white wedding with all the trimmings?"

"No, I don't think so," Andria shook her head. "If I decided on that Con would want to organise it, and honestly I don't think she's well enough, but we could manage a registry office one perfectly well ourselves, and all she'd have to do was come.

He looked at her for a moment, his eyes smiling, then he said quietly:

"You really are over it, aren't you? You've forgiven her completely."

"Yes, I have." A reluctant smile crossed Andria's face. "Perhaps I should be grateful to them both in a way, because if they hadn't behaved like that you and I wouldn't have met, and think how awful that would have been!"

"I think it's time for me to make a confession," Ellard said, his hand fondling

231

the back of her neck. "I loved you right from the start, Andy, and even if Oliver hadn't let you down, I'd have done everything I could to get you away from him short of knocking him over the head or abducting you. That's why I moved in so quickly when I heard what had happened — I didn't want you disappearing abroad somewhere where I couldn't trace you or getting yourself mixed up with some other guy on the rebound. And in case you're still in any doubt let me tell you that what I felt for Sheila was absolutely nothing compared to what I feel for you."

"I — I feel the same," Andria smiled back at him. "Ellard, can we start organising that wedding right away? Tomorrow, for instance?"

"The sooner the better." Ellard kissed her, long and lingeringly. "Darling, I must get a taxi for you, you'll be dead beat in the morning. I'll go and phone for one."

She joined him in the foyer, waiting while he dialled the number, sleepy now but buoyed up with deep happiness. Tonight she must be apart from Ellard, but for the last time — the future was theirs, stretching away before them, full of promise and excitement, and best of all, love . . .

THE END

TO FIGHT THE WILD
Rod Ansell and Rachel Percy

Lost in uncharted Australian bush, Rod Ansell survived by hunting and trapping wild animals, improvising shelter and using all the bushman's skills he knew.

COROMANDEL
Pat Barr

India in the 1830s is a hot, uncomfortable place, where the East India Company still rules. Amelia and her new husband find themselves caught up in the animosities which seethe between the old order and the new.

THE SMALL PARTY
Lillian Beckwith

A frightening journey to safety begins for Ruth and her small party as their island is caught up in the dangers of armed insurrection.